THE EXAMINED LIFE

The EXAMINED LIFE

VIRGIL JOSE

YELLOWBACK MYSTERIES
JAMES A. ROCK & COMPANY, PUBLISHERS
ROCKVILLE • MARYLAND

The Examined Life by Virgil Jose

is an imprint of JAMES A. ROCK & CO., PUBLISHERS

Address comments and inquiries to:

YELLOWBACK MYSTERIES
James A. Rock & Company, Publishers
9710 Traville Gateway Drive, #305
Rockville, MD 20850

E-mail:

jrock@rockpublishing.com   lrock@rockpublishing.com
Internet URL: www.rockpublishing.com

Paperback ISBN: 978-1-59663-569-2

Library of Congress Control Number: 2007928490

Printed in the United States of America

First Edition: 2007

To

Ellen, Jeanne,

Laura, Chris, Dolores,

Don and Bob

ACKNOWLEDGMENTS

My thanks to my longtime friends Donald Piché and Dr. Robert Hogan for reading my first draft and making invaluable suggestions; to Anne Dillon and Jean Foster Akin for their editing expertise; to my wife Jeanne for her help in manuscript preparation; to Dr. Ellen Bauerle for publishing me in an Ebook format; and to Jim Rock for publishing me in paperback

CHAPTER ONE

The year was 1987 in the month of May.

"A man's been killed. I think it might be David."

Gil Rodrigues sat in his little office, dazed, hearing the quavering voice on the phone pressed to his ear. He stared at his computer. He sat without moving. His heart began to race, his stomach fluttered.

Reflexively, he ran a shaking hand along his temple, where his dark hair carried signs of gray. Before him, on his computer screen, was a report he had been writing, recording his surveillance of an apparently healthy man faking total disability. The words of the report blurred before his eyes. He stared at them but saw nothing. *David couldn't be dead. Nancy never gets anything straight. It must be someone else.*

"Gil, did you hear me? Turn on Channel Two," the voice on the line directed him. It was his neighbor Nancy Abbott.

Gil answered her, but he later couldn't recall what he said to her. He sat in complete silence a moment, but did not hear the click on the line as his caller hung up.

He remained still, thinking of David alive, willing David alive. When Gil finally heard the off-hook alarm, he was startled to realize he was still clutching the handset. He put it back in the cradle.

Turning away from his report on the computer screen, he snapped on the small television set he used to review his surveillance tapes of persons suspected of insurance fraud.

An attractive Asian reporter stood in the middle of a tree-lined street. Her glossy black hair hung straight so as to brush the tops of her narrow shoulders. The caption at the bottom of the screen read, "Roseanne Chu Mobile TV News 2." Gil turned up the volume.

"We're in Los Altos Village, where a man was found dead—apparently shot—in his car about a block and a half from the Western Light Buddhist Temple, one of the largest such temples in the U.S. Residents we spoke to earlier told us street crimes of this nature are a rarity in this quiet bedroom community about twenty-five miles east of Los Angeles."

She paused for a moment to listen to some off-camera comments and then continued.

"We don't know the identity of the victim yet, but a bystander tells us he has seen the car a number of times and thinks it's owned by a man from here in the community. We'll try to get a sheriff's department spokesperson on camera shortly for some more information."

The scene had been cordoned off. Police and medical personnel milled in front of the vehicle where Gil assumed the body still lay. Roseanne Chu and her camera team had been positioned about ten yards from the officials working in and around the car. It was difficult to say for sure, with so much happening between where the reporter stood and where the car was parked, but Gil was almost certain he recognized David Chang's five-year-old Honda. It had been repainted with non-stock orange-yellow paint following an accident. The car on the screen was the same unmistakable saffron. Gil had teased David about his choice of colors, but David took no offense. He insisted good-naturedly that he liked it, and assured Gil it was just coincidence that the car's color matched the robes of the Buddhist monks and nuns—the people with whom

David associated as a practicing member of the Western Light Buddhist Temple.

Gil reminded himself, though, that he couldn't be sure this was David's car on the screen. Gil was a licensed private investigator—someone hired because of his ability to take his time and assess things objectively. If he had learned anything over the years, it was that things were not always as they appeared, that it was unwise to jump to conclusions before all the facts were in. Of course, he had long since learned that bad things happened to good people. He hoped he was wrong but he knew that this was probably David's body in that car. He shook his head, trying to dislodge the thought of David lying bloody and lifeless in his car on a public street, with strangers staring at him as if he were a museum exhibit draped with a plastic sheet.

Gil had become jaded over the years by news stories that had been given unmerited attention, and some days he found on-the-scene news so appalling he avoided it altogether. But today as he watched the news unfolding, he leaned forward, his dark brown eyes sharply focused on the images on the screen, trying to make sense of what had happened, amazed by how quickly a life could be snuffed out.

On this day a friend's death had become "breaking news" at mid-morning. And it was as freakish, as much like a circus, as any calamity he had ever seen exploited by local TV outlets.

Only days before he had watched a reporter waiting to ambush a young Los Angeles mother arriving home to find paramedics, police, and TV cameras on her front lawn. It was in this arena that the poor woman learned that her four-year-old son had been struck and killed by a speeding truck. The dead child's grandmother, who had overseen his care, was slumped against the front porch steps, trembling, eyes vacant, while paramedics draped her shoulders with a light blanket.

When Gil heard the mother's wail and saw her collapse into

the arms of neighbors, he averted his eyes and clicked to another channel.

But that was yesterday's anguish and yesterday's news. Life always went on, but today it was *his* friend in the news. Now it seemed that life had stopped altogether. Now the news reporter had Gil's full attention.

But still, Gil told himself that he couldn't be positive it was David. And he knew he wasn't going to drive to the scene and gawk with others. If the victim was his friend, Gil would hear soon enough, and he fought the impulse to call David's family. David's wife, daughter or sister would ring him here at the office, or at home, before nightfall. Unless, by some merciful coincidence, there was a second bright lemon-orange Honda in California that just happened to contain a dead man within three miles of David's home. Gil wouldn't count on that.

On the TV he noticed increased activity on the suburban street in Los Altos Village. For the most part, the cameraman kept the murder scene in the background of the shot. Technicians—"criminalists" as they now called themselves—collected crime scene evidence and took pictures. They wore disposable smocks, and Gil assumed they donned latex gloves and used tweezers to pick up small objects and put to them into clear plastic bags, which they labeled carefully with felt tip pens. He had seen his share of this kind of thing on the police dramas and similar on-scene news stories. The coroner's van had been moved nearly parallel to the scene. Two attendants in blue jumpsuits with the word CORONER stenciled on their backs stood by. They looked bored and were most likely waiting for instructions to remove the body from the car—the body that the persons in charge had mercifully shielded from the eyes of men and women on the street, and from the television audience. Gil crouched very close to the little television screen, to hear Roseanne Chu through the tinny speaker.

The scene Gil took in had a surreal aspect, like something

seen and heard in a dream. The little figures on the little screen all seemed to be moving in slow motion and he even made an effort at some lip-reading, but without success. From somewhere inside himself Gil sensed a pulling back, an impulse to flee, as if his mind and his body were trying to stop the flood of sights and sounds that now repelled him.

Onscreen, Ms. Chu had managed to corral a tall, composed sergeant from the sheriff's department and propel him into the spotlight. Small in stature, Chu was forced to thrust her microphone up into the man's face while he hunched down. Gil listened attentively to the man's words.

"At approximately 0815 hours this morning," the sergeant began, "a citizen reported a car parked in front of his home containing an adult male he described as Asian with a head wound and apparently dead."

In typical reporter style, Ms. Chu yanked the mike back to her own lips.

"Sergeant Piché, is your department ruling this a homicide or could it be suicide?" She snapped the microphone back into the sergeant's face.

"Well, no weapon has been located here at the scene, so a suicide appears unlikely. However, only the coroner can rule on the cause of death, so we can't say for sure at this point. With no weapon at the scene, a failed robbery or carjacking is always possible, but I'd prefer not to speculate further."

Ms. Chu cut in again, "Can you tell us if the victim lived here in town?"

"No, I'm sorry," Sergeant Piché replied. "The victim was tentatively identified through his driver's license, but we'll have to withhold his identity for now."

He straightened up and stepped back from the microphone as if he would walk away, but then leaned down again quickly, like a large bird pecking at a kernel of corn.

"Uh, as I said, we have no other information available at this time, but we ask anyone who might have information to contact the sheriff's department."

"Thank you. This is Roseanne Chu for KWBS in Los Altos Village. Now back to you, Frank." Then she was gone as the studio anchor summed up her coverage and reminded viewers that she would be reporting on ceremonies at the temple within the hour.

Gil turned off the set. He stared at the blank screen for a minute or two, thinking. Finally, and because he knew he had to, he turned back to the computer monitor and refocused his attention on the closing paragraph of his report. He could barely think right now, but he knew he had to wrap up this report and deliver it on time or risk losing a good client. He finished it, gave it a cursory proofread, printed it, and slipped it into an envelope with his invoice. The envelope was addressed to the claims manager who had hired him. He stamped the envelope "Confidential" and sealed it.

He took a deep breath, holding the envelope tightly in his hand. These jobs could be a bore, and it was his belief that any high school graduate could do them, but his profession paid the bills. As such, Gil was always obligated to finish jobs even if he wasn't in the mood—even, as in this case, if he was in a mild state of shock. His thoughts returned to the TV images he had seen. "Why in hell would anyone kill David?" He spoke the words aloud as he shut down his computer, then caught himself again and reminded himself that it just might be someone else, but that thought gave no consolation. He turned in his chair and looked at the wall. He would need an extra martini tonight.

Aside from the TV/VCR, FM/CD player, computer, cameras, and other electronic tools of his trade strewn about, Gil's office was austerely furnished with discount assemble-it-yourself furniture. Two plants that he wouldn't have been able to name with a gun to his head were badly in need of fertilizer and water. Between the browning plants lay a never-used ashtray, cut and hammered from an artillery shell casing. It was engraved with the words "Saigon 1961," and a cartoon-like character, who was wearing a cloak and fedora, and holding a dagger in one hand and a bolt of lightning in the other.

The few remaining items that represented Gil's identity hung on the wall of his "executive suite"—a two-hundred-fifty square-foot office with a two-by-three-foot window, for which he paid an additional twenty-five dollars per month rent. The window was sealed, and looked onto the blank wall of the building next door.

The office had only one extra chair, relatively comfortable, which Gil hardly ever needed because his practice rarely called for clients to visit his office. He used the chair to prop his feet on when he felt like taking a nap.

On the wall were three photos: his favorite picture of Helen, taken only months before she became ill; his daughter Laura at her law school's graduation and his son Chris at his Police Academy graduation. Next to those were Gil's master's degree from UCLA in history, and his PI license issued by the California Bureau of Security and Investigative Services. Both documents bore his birth name, Gilberto J. Rodrigues.

For the first time in months, Gil actually looked at his furnishings. He was glad that few people had ever set foot in here. The place needed dusting, the ceiling needed paint, and the rug definitely needed a good shampoo. If Helen had ever seen it in this condition, she would have had a fit. But he imagined himself explaining to her that the office was much like a monk's cell—humble, even sterile.

The only other item on the wall was a sign in a dime-store frame. It read: "The unexamined life is not worth living.—Socrates." And beneath that were the words: "The examined life ain't so hot either.—Anonymous."

The phone rang for the second time that day.

"Uncle Gil?" Sabrina Chang's voice was that of a young woman who had been weeping, but who had composed herself through an act of will.

"So," Gil said, "it *was* your dad after all."

"Yes." The "yes" was little more than a whisper.

"Damn it to hell," Gil said, slumping in his chair and pressing his palm to his suddenly damp forehead. "I can't believe this is happening … "

"I thought I recognized the car on the television news," Gil went on. "Sabrina, honey, I can't tell you how sorry I am."

Even through the phone, Gil sensed that the young woman had pulled herself together with this call to him in mind. The voice was subdued, but resolute.

"I had barely arrived at work when I got the call from Mom. I feel like someone just punched me in the face. I just can't believe this."

"I'm so stunned myself, I can hardly think, Sabrina."

There was a pause as they both took several shallow breaths.

Then Sabrina said, "The Chinese have a proverb: 'When the messenger of death arrives, all affairs cease.' Maybe that's because it's so hard to do anything else."

"What have you found out from the police so far?" Gil asked her.

She sighed, then said, "Lieutenant Hara said it might have been a botched carjacking attempt, but that doesn't make sense."

"Why so, honey? It seems to be the crime du jour, to judge by the crime reports."

"I'd agree," she said, "except that Dad's money was still in his wallet. And aren't these guys usually after luxury cars and a driver with a fat wallet or Rolex?"

"Of course," Gil offered. "It doesn't fit the model."

There was a moment of silence while Gil listened to Sabrina's soft breath in the receiver. Then she spoke again.

"And then -- according to Mom—Dad's been acting very odd these past few days," she said.

"How? What do you mean?"

"Mom told me he was doing work on his computer, late into the night. He'd begun closing himself in his office at home, as if he didn't want her to hear his phone conversations when she was in the kitchen, or if she was passing his door on her way to the living room."

"No, not like your dad, at all."

"And Mom says he was just very anxious and secretive these last few days. She says she thinks he was making plans to meet someone—I mean someone other than his usual friends at the temple."

"What do *you* think, Sabrina?'

"Only that I don't believe this crap about a car theft or robbery gone bad. It's nothing I can prove, but ... "

"But?"

"But I can't avoid the feeling it's all connected somehow to his job and maybe those creeps he worked for."

"Why do you think they're creeps, honey?"

"Oh, call it a woman's intuition, a feeling—whatever, but they're just two creepy guys. And then," she hesitated, "I mean, why did Dad take his briefcase with him? He was just going to his Thursday night study session at the temple. He'd never brought it before when he went to study sessions. He would just take his text and notebook."

"There are a lot of reasons a man like your dad would have his briefcase with him, Sabrina. It isn't the most unusual thing in the world. Did you tell Lieutenant Hara your thoughts on all this?"

"No. I didn't tell him because—well, I just have a *feeling*—and I don't have the kind of evidence that cops need."

"Evidence? Evidence of what?"

"I don't know," Sabrina sighed.

"Sabrina, honey. You're tired. After you've gotten some rest, you'll see things more clearly … " Gil was trying to comfort her, but he felt he sounded condescending. If Sabrina thought so too, she didn't say it.

When she didn't respond, Gil asked, "How's your mom? And Diana? How are they doing?"

"The sheriff's people left Mom a while ago. Two nuns from the Temple are with her now."

"And your Aunt Diana? At the hospital?"

"Aunt Diana is holding up okay and trying to help me keep Mom together.

"I'll call her," Gil said.

"No need to for now. I told her I was going to call you. She said to tell you not to worry about her for the moment. She said she'd talk to you later -- her O.R. staff is short on nurses. She doesn't want to leave until she re-arranges the work schedule for the O.R. and," Sabrina chuckled, "she told me to give you a big kiss for her."

"In that case, is there anything I can do for you and the family?"

"Yes. Yes, there is something you can do."

Sabrina's voice became solemn. Gil knew that she had cast her next sentence before she called him. Her words were measured in the delivery.

"Uncle Gil, you and your family practically adopted my parents when they came here from China. My parents and I adored Helen. Your daughter Laura and I are close friends. You knew my dad, and what a sweet man he was."

"He and your Mom both," Gil said.

Then he heard her draw a breath before she said, "You asked if there's anything you can do? There is."

She paused before her next words.

"Find out who did this."

Gil barely waited for Sabrina to finish making her request. "Whoa, Sabrina! You know cops don't like civilians—especially PI's—butting into their investigations. And you know I don't do felony work. If you want a good felony PI, I can help you find a retired homicide detective, maybe even someone who is, say, ex-FBI. I'm talking about good guys—and a hell of a lot better than me for this kind of stuff."

Sabrina's voice was firm. "I'm sure you have plenty of good connections, Uncle Gil, but I'm also pretty sure we wouldn't be able to afford any of them. Besides, this is personal, and you … " she paused, "you're *family*."

"I know, Sabrina," he said, feeling a wave of emotion that made his throat tighten and his eyes become moist. "But we both have to be realistic."

Sabrina cut him off. She knew just what buttons to push and she had her emotions on hold to deliver the line that Gil saw coming. "Chinese don't use 'uncle' or 'auntie' for people outside of the family unless those people are special. I know my dad made sure you knew that."

Gil was silent for a full half-minute, but it seemed much longer. He knew Sabrina was waiting for him to speak. He wanted to help her and her family any way he could, but *this?* He had never investigated a murder, if that's what this was.

"Okay, maybe I can do some snooping around, but just snooping—no more, because I'd be in over my head. That's all I can promise. I know Lieutenant Hara. Let me talk to him before I make any more promises. I don't want to get your expectations too high."

"You'll do your best, Uncle Gil."

There was a beep on the line.

"Oh, wait a minute, Uncle, I have a call coming in."

He waited, listening to the void at the other end of the line. Then Sabrina was back. "It's the funeral director. This morning he said he'd call the Coroner to get some idea of when they'll release Dad's body. We'll talk later. And Uncle Gil … ?"

"Yes, honey."

"Find out who did this."

"Bye, Sabrina—and please, if there's anything more I can do, anything, let me know."

Gil hung up, not sure if she heard his last words. He put his hands in his lap, took a deep breath and closed his eyes.

When he felt a bit more collected, he picked up his report and left the office.

"When the messenger of death arrives, all affairs cease." He repeated Sabrina's words to himself and hoped he wouldn't regret his commitment to her.

CHAPTER TWO

Preoccupied with David, Gil delivered his report in person to his client, the Solar State Employers Insurance Company. Adam Koenig, the claims manager who gave Gil his assignments, would always make Gil sit and listen to a harangue that never varied: a venting of Koenig's hatred of the insurance cheats he called "minority types," by which he meant blacks, Hispanics, and people from the Middle East. Nor did Koenig care for their lawyers, whom he called "ambulance chasers," as if he had coined the term.

Koenig was a graduate of one of the many private, for-profit law schools in California. After law school, he learned quickly that the "white shoe firms" looked down on blue-collar lawyers and so, with a family to support, he had taken a job as a claims adjuster, a job that was once the province of high-school graduates. His hard work, education and bar membership, however, had served to put him on a fast track to a position of claims manager where he would remain until retirement. Daily exposure to claims that were inflated, if not outright fraudulent, could turn any essentially decent man into a confirmed cynic, which is what Koenig had, to his detriment, become.

Gil always listened politely to Koenig's tirades because eventually Koenig would wind down, scribble approval on the invoice and give Gil some new assignments. Gil would then hand-deliver his invoice to Shirley, in the accounts payable department, on the way out.

Gil treated Shirley with almost courtly civility, because the Shirleys of this world, Gil knew, had a way of sidetracking invoices from "vendors" who failed to treat them with the great deference they felt they, and their office, deserved.

Koenig had tried to mooch a lunch off Gil, as he did every time Gil came in to get paid, but Gil had begged off with an excuse fabricated on the spot. Gil himself had tried to take Shirley to lunch once, only to stay on her good side, but she had firmly let him know that it was against the rules to accept "gifts or favors" from people who were doing business with the company.

That had been okay with Gil. It saved on expenses and he found Shirley obnoxious anyway. He imagined watching her make four trips to the salad bar and having to listen to her struggles with her ex was an ordeal that he was only too happy to avoid.

It was only mid afternoon, but Gil was finding it hard to focus his attention. He really didn't have anything important to do for the rest of the day, and that was just as well. If he had to, he wouldn't have been able to focus on any task of substance anyway. He was avoiding the return home, and he knew it, and he knew why.

On his way home, he would have to avoid his favorite watering hole, because he knew that if he stopped there, given everything that had gone down, he would be tempted to have more than his usual two. Coupled with this, he didn't want to hear the talk and speculation about David's murder that would invariably be forthcoming from the bar's patrons, some of whom had been David's neighbors and acquaintances.

Gil was in conscious denial; he didn't want to think about David right now. He preferred to distract himself with busy routine. He pulled his Nissan into a While-U-Wait—his car was due for an oil change—overdue, actually, by about three thousand miles.

Gil then made a stop at Office Depot, spending another thirty minutes browsing, finally buying only an inkjet cartridge and a ream of paper. When Helen was alive he had never avoided going home, nor had he wanted to, but on this day The Gray One had struck down a dear friend and Gil's empty house was the last place he wanted to be. Finally, he stepped up to it and drove home, dreading what he knew would likely be the first of many sleepless nights.

The cat greeted him at the door, and then paced between his feet and the kitchen, demanding dinner. Nadia had been Helen's cat, and Gil had promised his wife that he would take care of the animal after she died. He opened a can of diced chicken, dumped it into Nadia's dish, and gave her a quick scratch on her cheeks and head. She acknowledged his attention by turning up her chin, closing her eyes and purring. It was a consoling sound, and Gil began rubbing the cat's throat until she decided she had enough and began picking at the food in her dish.

Gil rose and pulled a beer from the refrigerator. He picked up a newspaper and only half read a story about President Reagan's health, rumored to be failing since the assassination attempt six years past.

Then he parked in a recliner and busied his mind with trivial matters. He should call a housepainter. He should paint the house himself. The house was too big for him. It was haunted. He should sell it and move to a condo. He should trim the hedges. He should take a vacation. He should stay home. Gil threw the newspaper to the floor with enough force to startle the cat, and then put his head back and closed his eyes.

He didn't want to think of David as dead. Gil knew that he would continue to be in some level of denial until after the funeral, but questions lay in wait behind the denial: how well had he really known David? For that matter, how well do any of us know anyone? What did he know about David's job or his employers? And just what business had David actually been in?

Gil lay with his eyes closed and as he drifted off to sleep, he reflected that the beer had had some value after all. He felt the cat jump on to his lap, but that was the last he remembered until the phone woke both him and the cat.

It was his daughter.

"Hi, Laura. So you've heard? I figured you were in court, so I was going to call later."

"That's okay. Sabrina called me. It's just awful. It's one thing to deal with crimes among strangers, but this? Is there anything we can do to help?"

"Sabrina already asked me to see what I can do, but I'm not sure if I can do anything. You still seeing that lawyer from the other office—what was his name—Ralph?"

"It didn't work, but we're still friends." Laura quickly changed the subject back to David's murder. "Are you going to play Sam Spade on this one?"

"I promised Sabrina that I'd do a little digging around, but just to appease her and her mom. Homicide's not my bag. I think it's better to let others handle this."

"Just the same, Dad, I for one wouldn't want you on my tail for killing a friend of yours. I think your son would agree with me."

"Speaking of Chris, you want me to tell him or will you?"

"Already told him. He's on duty. I'm sure we'll see him at the funeral." With that, his daughter said a quick good-bye and hung up.

Gil pondered for a moment before drifting back to sleep. He slept fitfully and awoke frequently. He tried to read when he woke up, even to watch some nighttime television but it was, as usual, dreadful fare.

He changed to a different cable channel that was running a documentary on the Battle of Midway, which featured gun camera footage as well as scenes of sailors and airmen standing on carrier decks and manning anti-aircraft guns. Even in his half-sleep, Gil marveled at the courage and gallantry of the men who, captured on celluloid, were seemingly forever young. He wondered how many were still alive and had survived to marry and sire children.

He finally fell back to sleep in his chair and awoke as the first rays of sunlight streamed into the window. Nadia was pacing for her breakfast.

As usual, he welcomed the day with a three-mile jog, the exercise that gave him his energy and cleared his head. He did his lightweight workout and some crunches, and after a long shower he felt alert.

He brewed himself coffee from the mix of "all-purpose grind" he had bought on sale. He mixed it with some espresso to give it character and make it taste like an expensive brand. He tasted the orange juice. Finding it sour, he dumped it in the sink, then found two eggs in the fridge. He scrambled and slathered them with some industrial-strength salsa, hoping that none of the food contained the seeds of food poisoning. A stale English muffin tasted all right toasted and drenched in margarine.

Gil lingered over his coffee, giving the *LA Times* a quick scan, but absorbed little of what he read. His thoughts shifted between aversion and preoccupation. His reluctance gradually turned to resolve, with some feelings of doubt. "I'm not a homicide cop," he thought, "so where do I go from here?"

He'd learned from his days as a student of history that the simplest explanation of events would usually turn out to be the correct one. He was at least that much an intellectual, but he would have been embarrassed to have been called such. He simply tried never to read mystery into the mundane. It had been proven that Egyptian peasants were capable of moving a ten-ton stone with nothing more than some ropes, logs, and muscle. There was no need to posit that space aliens had been the builders of the pyramids. Ergo, Sabrina's dislike of her father's employers didn't make them murderers. That theory would have to go on a back burner, at least until the simpler explanations could be ruled out.

Gil decided to call the *Los Angeles Times* archival service and ask for a synopsis of every carjacking case chronicled in the past six months. He'd start there, anyway, and see where it led him. The *Times* couldn't possibly have reported every case, but the likelihood of it having reported the ones involving guns or violence was high. He requested the synopses be faxed to his office. For that he had to provide a credit card number, which he did while hoping that he wasn't over his limit.

When he arrived at his office, the news items from the paper lay in a heap on the floor under his fax machine. He had never bothered to install the copy tray on the machine because every bit of space was precious in such a cramped office, and he didn't need another item to bump into with his knees.

The *Times* had reported nine carjackings within the prior six months. Gil assembled the stories in chronological order. Only three were of interest to him. Gil scratched a matrix on a yellow pad and began making tick marks.

The carjackings had six features in common: The carjacker had used a handgun. He operated within a five-mile radius of David's murder. He had accosted his victims in the parking lots of shopping plazas. He had held his weapon to the victim's head or neck. He had forced his victims to drive to a residential area. And, last, but not least, he carjacked older models of Hondas because, as each story pointed out, they were especially prized by "chop shops" for the resale value of their parts.

The victims had described the carjacker as a male Hispanic in his late teens, sporting gang tattoos. They described his handgun as "small," with a narrow muzzle opening, which meant it could have been a .22 caliber. The problem was, the carjackings had taken place in more than one jurisdiction, potentially diluting efforts to catch the perpetrator.

With luck and some common sense, maybe the identification of David's killer would turn out to be a matter of some diligent and routine police work on the part of Sheriff's Lieutenant Steve Hara and his people. Gil felt selfish thinking this way, but the sooner the killer was caught, the sooner he, and David's family, could get on with their lives. He was eager to hear some encouraging news from Hara the next day.

CHAPTER THREE

David's murder had occurred less than two blocks from the Buddhist temple, one of the largest outside of Asia. Barely three lifetimes after the first Christian Mission was founded in nearby San Gabriel, the Western Light Temple had been built with the money of wealthy Taiwanese and other Chinese benefactors and it had quickly become a tourist Mecca for both Buddhists and non-Buddhists.

The crime had taken place in a community not yet granted cityhood, a fact that brought it under the jurisdiction of the Los Angeles County Sheriff.

The coroner had not yet released David's body, thereby delaying the funeral. Release was expected with a day or two at most, allowing David's family to make final funeral arrangements. In the meantime, Gil moved ahead with his own inquiries. He would treat Sabrina as his client.

Lieutenant Steve Hara was in charge of the investigation. He lived in the community and he and Gil had become friendly when their wives were teachers at the same elementary school. The four of them had often met for lunch, dinner, or backyard barbecues.

Lieutenant Hara was a third-generation Japanese-American—a "Sansei"—and a USC graduate. His father had served with distinction as an infantry officer in the Korean Conflict, a fact Steve mentioned at every opportunity. Steve was also an increasingly rare bird—a native Californian. His grandparents had been Central Valley farmers who, with his parents, had been placed in internment camps during WWII.

Gil and Steve had agreed to meet at the China Mandarin Restaurant. Gil had to specify which one, because it was part of a small chain in the San Gabriel Valley.

Gil arrived at the restaurant a few minutes early. Seated by himself, he was the recipient of several curious glances. People did tend to notice Gil. He was over six feet and had learned to stand tall because a high school gym teacher, an ex-marine, demanded that Gil and his classmates do so. Exercise kept Gil's body trim and his hair bore streaks of silver, which seemed to make people take him seriously. His warm, brown eyes and easy smile were effective in disarming the people whose cooperation he needed in his work.

When Lieutenant Hara arrived, he slid into Gil's booth beneath a panel of four mother-of-pearl tableaus in black enamel frames. Each tableau featured aristocratic Chinese women in elaborately detailed costumes, with the Great Wall in the background.

"Anne and I were talking about Helen just the other day" Hara said. "She and the other teachers miss her a lot. Still hard to believe she's gone. How long now … couple of years?"

"Just about, Steve—couple of years."

"It must still hurt, I'd guess."

"Yes, but the pain seems to have a half-life of about a year. Probably never does get to zero."

"Like some kind of radioactive stuff? I like the analogy, but you came here to learn something about David Chang, and don't need me scaring up your ghosts." Hara paused and then stumbled over his words. "If I may—that is, if it's not too, uh, personal—how are things with you and Diana? Think you'll be heading to a wedding chapel soon?"

"I don't mind the question, Steve. We're still an item, but we haven't talked about marriage."

The waitress brought a pot of tea. No liquor license here. The two men ordered the sweet and sour shrimp, a lunch special that became a dinner entree after three for an extra two dollars.

Gil sipped his tea and paused for a long moment. "Steve, let me be frank. After you talked to David's daughter, she got the impression that you folks are looking at her dad's murder as some random street crime."

"And that's based on what I had to say to the press, besides 'no leads' or 'we haven't a clue.' Anyway, what does she have in mind—a mob hit? Why would a professional hit man do someone like David Chang? Does she know something that we don't?"

"Nothing she could take to you or to court, Steve. She can't stand the men her dad worked for. According to her, David was acting funny for days before he was killed and she believes he was on his way to meet someone when he died. His wallet was found on his body and her gut feeling tells her his death may be related somehow to his work."

"And he evidently met friends there at the temple. Is that your understanding, too?" Hara refilled their teacups. "I regarded David as an acquaintance, but you knew him pretty well, I believe."

"Yes. Apparently David went there at least once a week to meet with some sort of study group in one of their conference rooms. He once told me that they have the biggest library on Buddhism in the western hemisphere. Devout Buddhist David didn't go there to socialize."

"If his daughter has some evidence ... "

"Steve, if she had solid evidence she'd bring it to you. She's not stupid. Can't you tell me anything at all that wasn't in the paper?"

Hara sat up and stared past Gil as if reading off a teleprompter. His voice was muted as he spoke. "Body discovered probably within hours of death. Sitting behind the wheel, a .22 caliber bullet in the base of the skull."

"Silencer? Witnesses? Fingerprints?" Gil pressed for more.

"No silencer needed. Powder burns suggest the muzzle was placed against his flesh, which acts much like a silencer in that case. Death occurred instantly. No prints other than those of the victim and his family. We've been interviewing anyone we know who might have been in the area at the time, but it's tough with the influx of so many immigrants."

"Yes—fear, distrust of police, authorities in general. I run into it in my work all the time," Gil said. "Maybe the monks or nuns could encourage their members to come forward if they know something."

"My detective on the case, Robert Chin, speaks Mandarin. You'd think that would be a big advantage, but it doesn't work that way. Because he was born here, they regard him as just another American who just happens to have a Chinese face."

"Has he learned anything so far?"

"As far as we know, David was seen in the temple parking lot by a member of his study group, but he never showed up inside the temple."

"That's interesting."

"You bet. That's why carjacking isn't out of the question. Hondas, especially older ones, are one of the most stolen cars in the country."

"So you're saying, Steve, that someone could have made him drive a couple of blocks, where they killed him for his car? But then why didn't the killer take the car?"

"He'd have to shove the body out, and he could have gotten spooked with a car driving by, or some voices—anything. There's plenty of precedents for this type of a crime being botched, with the perp taking off without the car."

"Steve—just out of idle curiosity, mind you—I checked out some recent news stories on carjackings in the general area. Considering that at least three might fit a similar pattern, I'd have to agree that we—you—can't rule carjacking out."

These frustrating realities caused both men to fall silent, and neither looked at the other for several minutes while they ate. Each waited for the other to break the silence.

Gil finally did. "Steve, let's cut the crap. Okay, so you don't have any solid clues yet, but what's your gut feel?"

"Gut feel? Off the record?" Hara took a deep breath and jumped right in again. "My sense is that your friend was murdered by someone he either knew and trusted—or knew well enough to think that his life wasn't in jeopardy. But, mind you, I'm not ruling out a botched carjacking yet."

"The victim puts up an argument, or struggles, and the carjacker loses his cool and shoots." Gil pointed his finger like a pistol.

"That's my point. It's not at all far-fetched. We've had several incidents over the past three or four months where the victims were able to walk away. Some who were gun-savvy described small caliber handguns."

"Sounds like the stories I found in the Times. In principle I have to agree, Steve. But I'm getting a sense that the shooter must have been in the back seat. That sounds more likely."

"Yes, but he didn't have to be. He could have been left-handed, and yet even if he wasn't, that doesn't guarantee he wasn't in the front passenger seat."

"Maybe there were two of them? One got in the car with David. The other followed in a second car?"

"Very possible, maybe likely. Lots of carjackings are pulled off by a team of two guys, so I just can't rule that out at this time either," Hara said.

"One would almost think a mob hit," Gil said, "but I couldn't imagine David doing anything that would make him a target of wiseguys."

"From the little I know about your friend, Gil, I would tend to agree, but it does have elements of a professional hit. You asked for my hunch and you got it, but it's too early yet to surmise either motive or suspect."

"Maybe I'm grabbing at straws, Steve, but could it be mistaken identity?"

"I can't rule out anything, Gil, especially after that case in New Jersey. Solid citizen whacked in what police knew had to be a mob hit, but they couldn't figure it out. There were no loans from sharks, no gambling, drugs, or wife chasing—the usual things leading up to a hit. Mob guys just don't hit civilians for no good reason."

"You're talking about the hit in New Jersey, about two years ago? Long Branch, was it – 'down the shore'—as they say? Victim was visiting a hospital. Turned out he was a ringer for a mob guy who was supposed to be visiting another wiseguy in the same hospital."

"One and the same. You're from New Jersey aren't you, Gil?"

"From the Portugee section of Newark, born and raised."

"Newark Portugee who did a scholarship to UCLA. No wonder you're such a wise ass." Hara wore a wide smirk.

They both grinned. "Yes, we're talking about the same case, Gil," Hara continued. It took a year for the cops to piece it together. The guy was in the wrong place at the wrong time. Poor bastard had the bad luck not just to resemble a wiseguy, but a wiseguy with a contract on him."

Gil's words were barely above a whisper. "Man, I'd like to burn the sonofabitch who did this to David."

"We all want him, Gil." Hara's tone was now what he would use when talking to a subordinate. "Don't do anything to jeopardize your license. I know more about you than you may realize."

"Oh, you know about the ax murders?" It was Gil's turn to smirk. "But the doctors told me to take my meds and put my past behind me."

"Always the wise ass, Gil. Fact is, I met people at your wife's funeral who knew you when."

"Stories grow in the retelling," Gil said. "They take on a life of their own."

Hara's tone became matter-of-fact. "I don't know about that. One knew you in Vietnam, another when you boxed in Golden Gloves and killed a man in your last fight. The rap is you had a left hook that would fell a mule. Is that why we've never seen the two belts you won?"

"That was an accident. I left my trophies with my parents years ago. Haven't seen them since and never tried to find them. My parents have been gone for a long time now."

"Deaths in the ring are always accidents. I hope it's not still eating you."

"I knew him from the neighborhood. Nobody, not even his family, blamed me, but it's something I'd rather not think about."

"I guess we all have our ghosts, but I've got to remind you not to play TV private eye and get yourself into trouble. Interfering with my investigation of a capital crime could get your tit in a ringer. If you pick up on anything, you come to me first now, hear?"

"Steve … " Gil paused before formulating his question. "A professional hit doesn't have to be mob only, correct?"

"You're saying that there are lots of people running around such as ex-military, law enforcement, etc., who could pull off a professional-type hit?"

"Exactly."

Hara shrugged. "Yes, of course, if you're of the 'anything's possible' school of thought. I'd guess we have as least a half-dozen former Green Berets, SEALS, Rangers and the like in the Sheriff's Department alone. Lots of those types running around these days but with David's murder, it just widens the field and creates more speculation, without any solid suspect or evidence. Hunches and intuitions are okay, but speculation is worthless when solving a crime."

Gil rolled his eyes. "You're right, Steve, and here I'm the guy preaching simple explanations over the far-fetched. It just *seems* so damned professional with no prints or other conventional clues."

"I agree, Gil, but I've got Chin working on it almost exclusively. Doesn't take long for a case to get cold and I want to avoid that if I can."

Gil said nothing. He had heard all he needed to for now. He signaled the waitress to bring the check, then handed her cash before she could set her little tray on the table. He offered a handshake to Hara before parting.

"Give your sweet wife my affections, Steve. She was one of Helen's buds and that makes her one of mine. Oh—and before I forget—Sabrina did say that her dad took his briefcase with him when he left the house that day."

"Thanks, we'll cover that in our interviews. I don't recall one being around the scene. And one more time, Gil, don't get yourself in trouble."

"Who me?" Gil smiled. "Sayonara, Stevo-san."

CHAPTER FOUR

Gil allowed his son to drive him and his daughter to the cemetery and chapel in Alhambra, a community with a large Asian population on the eastern border of Los Angeles. Their car pulled into the chapel's parking lot several minutes before David's small funeral cortege arrived from the funeral home in LA's Chinatown. Gil stood with his son and daughter outside the chapel, in the shade of a pepper tree. They barely looked at each other and said nothing. As it was impossible to stand in a cemetery on a partly cloudy day and avoid at least a passing thought of one's own mortality, all three were conscious of what the other two were thinking.

The variety of styles and sheer number of grave markers and headstones indicated that this was an older cemetery and, as such, nearly full. The vegetation was decades old, and while the pine trees needed trimming, the lawn and numerous bird of paradise flowers and hydrangeas seemed well tended. The fence was completely obscured with ivy. Some tree roots had begun to lift and even crack some of the older grave markers, but it was unlikely that the families of those lying beneath these markers ever came here anymore.

It had been a quiet and peaceful place when it had opened in the late forties, but commercial buildings and road traffic now hemmed it in on all four sides, and it had become an island in an industrial park. That day one heard the sounds of birds, which clashed with the hum of road traffic outside the gates. It occurred to Gil that these older and full cemeteries, coupled with the rising price of grave plots, accounted for the increasing practice of cremation. They had cremated Helen in accordance with her wishes and his ashes would lie next to hers in the veterans' cemetery in due time.

Gil had witnessed Buddhist funeral services in Vietnam, but this was his first since then and the first ever for his kids. The service was conducted mostly in Mandarin. Gil, his son and daughter, and other non-Asian mourners had to take their cues from the others as to when to sit or stand during the service, which was held in the chapel.

The ceremony concluded, and after some additional prayers at the door of the crematorium, only David's wife Mei, his sister , his daughter Sabrina, Buddhist holy men and the funeral director were permitted to follow David in his coffin into the red brick crematorium with its factory-style chimney. There, after final prayers, David's coffin would be left with attendants who would transfer the body to a cardboard coffin before committing it to the fiery furnace that returns flesh to dust.

While Gil was acquainted with most of the mourners, neighbors of the Changs, he had never met any of David's colleagues until that day. In the milling about that follows a funeral service, two suited Chinese men approached Gil in a file that Gil assumed was in order of rank. The lead man spoke English with a British accent.

"Mr. Rodrigues," he began with a half-smile that revealed even but smoke-stained teeth. "I am Zhiyuan—Jeff—Ming. This is Dewei—Jerry—Liao."

Each proffered a business card with their right hand cupped in the left as if holding something precious. They then shook hands, in turn, with Gil, with three measured pumps apiece, and bowed slightly as they did so. Gil smiled as he noted that, of the two men, only Ming seemed to know how to match suit, tie, shirt, belt and shoes.

"We understand you are a close friend of the Changs." Ming's speech was measured and a little formal. "I am president of the DaleeAhn Corporation. Mr. Liao is our vice president. You may already be aware that David was our accountant."

Gil forced himself to be polite. "It's good of you to be here."

"This is a terrible loss for David's family, Mr. Rodrigues. It's also a terrible loss for our business. We trust the authorities will determine who took his life."

"That's the least we can hope for, Mr. Ming. David was a saint."

For a moment, Ming's face betrayed a hint of a smirk, before changing to an expression of studied solemnity. His voice took on a tone of righteous anger. "In China, the assassin would be shot, much as he took the life of his victim."

Gil decided to play it straight. He looked to be sure David's family was out of earshot. "If you have any ideas of who might have wanted to kill David … "

Ming jumped in. "We would call the authorities immediately."

"Pleased to meet you, Mr. Ming. Will we see you at the luncheon arranged by David's family?"

"I would hope you would call me Jeff. Why yes, but we may not be able to stay long. It will be good to meet David's friends and neighbors."

"Then I guess we'll see you there in awhile." Gil said it with a tone empty of any inflection.

As Ming turned and walked away with his colleague, Gil sensed a cultivated physical strength and an athletic quality in the man not palpable in Liao, who otherwise resembled an out-of-shape Asian businessman. Ming walked like a jock, with feet close to the ground and with an erect back and neck. Gil saw Ming take those momentary, but deliberate looks at the people and events in the immediate area—a habit usually acquired through some type of training. Like Gil, he was a man always acutely aware of his surroundings. Liao walked like a man old before his time. Both men lit cigarettes right away.

Gil's car was facing in the direction of the chimney of the crematorium. Without a word, Gil and his kids cast a long, parting gaze at that red brick chimney as they entered the car. In the California morning sun, little mirage-like convection currents were now visible at the chimney top and the muffled rumble of ignited gas jets became audible.

Although they didn't say it, Gil and his kids felt relieved that the luncheon for the mourners wasn't to be held at David's house. It was better for the family, if not the guests, to be away from the physical reminders of David in life if only for an hour or two. They would have to deal with their grief and reminders of him for the rest of their lives and they seemed to take some comfort in the expressions of condolences from everyone, especially the non-Asians who had become their good friends and neighbors.

The luncheon was held at the Lok Tin Chinese restaurant. Gil and his late wife had eaten there on occasion with David and his wife. Each time David liked to point out that "Lok Tin" meant "heaven's gate" in English.

Gil sat across from his son at a table surrounded mostly by men. Gil had heard most of his son's cop anecdotes, but the other men, hearing them for the first time, seemed to enjoy them.

Sabrina and Gil's daughter had some catching up to do. They hadn't seen each other all that much since high school and college. And they now saw less of each other since Sabrina was off in the world of engineering and Laura in the world of law.

Watching them, Gil couldn't help but admire the two young women. Both were as pretty as any young film actress. Better still, both were intelligent and educated, competent and independent.

That Gil could hear nothing of their conversation was of no consequence. Somewhere in the back of his mind was the awareness that some day they would be sitting like this in a similar place and discussing his own death. But for now Gil pushed that thought from his mind, because after the solemnity of David's funeral, it was a joy to watch them—pretty, young, animated and laughing now and then at some girly joke, the content of which he would never know.

David's widow Mei and sister Diana were sitting among friends who spoke mostly Mandarin, with an occasional foray into English for the benefit of the non-speakers who were drawn into their conversation now and then.

Ming and Liao sat among David's Asian friends and some Buddhist nuns in their saffron robes. Liao seemed to say little when he wasn't stuffing his face, but Ming was playing the charming and worldly conversationalist, a role in which he was both comfortable and competent. Gil's first impression of the man was of someone educated and articulate, if not cultured in the literary sense. His English was nearly flawless and had to be the result of years of study and practice. Gil had to assume that such training was reserved only for the privileged, maybe ruling class, members of Ming's native society.

Gil observed him without staring. He reminded himself that Sabrina seemed convinced that Ming was connected to her father's murder, but her conviction was, admittedly, based on intuition coupled with her dislike of the two men. She was, after all, American through and through. She was also first generation and Gil, who grew up among immigrants, knew that first generation kids often harbored an embarrassment about those from the "old country" with their accents and un-American customs, and that outlook could color Sabrina's perception of events. Gil didn't want to believe that David's killer could be in this room at this very moment, but he knew that he would have to keep an open mind if he were going to be of any help in finding David's killer.

Here in this setting, Gil felt some misgivings having committed his efforts on behalf of David and his family. Gil led a simple life after Helen died. He was paying his bills and—thanks to David's playing the matchmaker—had recently begun seeing Diana Chang. He was sure, when digging up the news stories on carjackings in the area, that he was merely duplicating the work of Hara's people. And a PI who needed an occasional favor from the local sheriff's station didn't need the officer in charge annoyed with him for getting involved in a matter as serious as murder. Why complicate his life now by doing what should be left to the sheriff?

But other thoughts eclipsed the doubts and hardened his resolve. Gil knew that dozens of murders remained unsolved each year in any given metropolitan area. And, in David's death, there seemed to be none of the evidence that police and prosecutors needed to catch and convict the killer in the short term. Gil felt sure that, without a major break like witnesses or standard pieces of evidence such as fingerprints, David's case would become a "cold case" quickly. That meant that if he were to do anything to solve the murder, he had to act quickly, too.

Guests began to leave. Gil watched one man say his goodbyes to David's family. As the man spoke, Gil noticed Mei and Diana looking his way, making brief eye contact as they did so. It was apparent that the man had asked them to point Gil out.

Instead of going straight to the door, the man walked toward Gil's table. He wore a forced smile. "Mr. Rodrigues, we have never met, but my name is Richard Heng. I have known David and his family now for a number of years."

Gil stood to shake the man's hand. The gesture seemed to make the man self-conscious if only because Gil stood a head taller. "Nice to meet a friend of David's," said Gil. "We're all a bit numb, I believe."

"Please sit down, Mr. Rodrigues." The man continued to look uneasy. "I can't stay, but may I have your business card? I wish to talk to you about something, but this is not the time or place."

Gil pulled a card from his wallet. The man's anxiety touched Gil such that he wrote his home number on the card before giving it to the man. "And may I have your card, Mr. Heng?"

The man made a patting gesture over his jacket pockets. "I don't have any with me. I'm sorry. I must go. I will call you, Mr. Rodrigues."

"May I have your phone number?" Gil reached for a pen, but the man ignored him and left hurriedly, giving a quick wave goodbye to those people remaining.

When it came time for Gil to make his exit, he made a point of asking Sabrina about Heng. Sabrina had no idea of what Heng might want to speak with Gil about and knew Heng only as a friend of her dad's. She suggested that her mom might know, but Gil's instincts told him to let it lie for now.

Diana Chang was standing with Sabrina, Mei, and some other mourners saying their goodbyes. When Gil made eye contact with her, she nodded toward a corner of the room near the waiters' station. Gil told his kids to meet him at the car and he followed Diana to where she waited near some carts and empty tables out of earshot of those remaining.

"Gil, sweetie, thanks for all you're doing. I … "

Gil cut her off. "But I haven't done anything yet except show up today."

"Sabrina said you promised to help find the person who took David from us."

"Yes, I did." Gil took a deep breath and added, "And, my dear, to be frank. I'm already having second thoughts about that promise."

Diana took Gil's hand. "It might be a couple of weeks before we can get together again. I'm understaffed at the hospital and we've got a state inspection coming up."

"And whatever time off you do have you'll want to spend with Mei. She'll be grateful." Gil squeezed her hand slightly, and then pressed her fingertips to his lips.

"Thanks, again." Her eyes were moist. "David thought the world of you and Helen."

She then took his tie between her thumb and forefinger, pulled him slightly foreword and kissed him on the cheek. It was a long, lingering kiss—the kind that would mark them as lovers to any observer. She backed away slightly with her eyes fixed on his and without another word wiped the lipstick off his cheek and walked to the door, leaving him to trail several feet behind her.

Gil's kids had to return to their jobs, so he let them drop him off at his office where he had left his car. The three paused before parting and looked at each other silently for about a half minute. His son's lips were pursed. "Dad, it's awful. First mom and now David." He shook his head.

Gil embraced his son and then his daughter who kissed his cheek and looked at the ground.

"I can't thank you enough for coming and for your help today."

"Dad, don't even mention it. We'll see you soon, " said Laura.

Gil watched them as they got into their car, and then waved as they pulled away.

Gil could easily have gotten Heng's address and phone number from any number of sources, but the man's obvious unease told Gil to let the man come forward when he felt comfortable in so doing. Common sense dictated that friends, relatives and business associates would be the best place to start investigating a murder, so Gil had to hope the man knew something or could point him in the right direction. Gil would give the man a day or two to get in touch. It was clear that Heng had something to get off his chest, but had to feel at ease in doing so. And, if the man didn't call, Gil would find him.

CHAPTER FIVE

Gil barely slept that night. For certain he needed his jog the next morning. It kept the blues away after Helen. It also kept his half-century-old body in good health.

He got up at 6 A.M., did his weights first and then began his jog though his residential neighborhood. Exercise usually cleared his mind, but today Gil found himself bedeviled by the pitiable indignity of David's death.

"Execution-style" was the phrase reporters and cops liked to use in these cases. What had David ever done to deserve that, Gil wondered. A montage of grainy news photos and black-and-white newsreels whirred past his mind's eye. Those images had imprinted themselves on the sponge-brain of his childhood years before he or any of his neighbors had TV. It had been the newsreels and photos in magazines such as *Life* that had given him and his young friends their first breath-catching glimpses of controlled violence in a world outside of their childhood, a childhood that had never seen war first hand.

The pictures of dead soldiers and civilians of World War II, the trials of Nazis and Japanese generals and the pictures of their unspeakable crimes had been burned into Gil's memory. As an adult, he had seen victims of combat, yet that violence was no greater part of his consciousness than those images of violence first glimpsed, in childhood, on paper. At this point in life, those secondhand images seemed more real than the realities he had witnessed firsthand.

He knew it was customary for the Russians and Chinese to dispose of unwanted citizens with a bullet in the base of the brain or through the heart from behind. Newsmagazines carried photos of public executions in China. The condemned, arms bound, were driven to the killing ground in open trucks. Often, before execution, they were paraded before thousands of onlookers in stadiums. This was deemed "humane" as if any kind of violent death were humane.

Of one thing Gil was certain: David's troubles were over. As quickly as the thought entered Gil's mind, he was annoyed with himself for thinking such. Thoughts like these wasted time. Worse, they deferred action. It was time to turn his energies to finding David's killer or killers. And if he didn't feel up to the task, Gil owed it to Sabrina, her mother and aunt to say so.

Back at his office Gil had to take care of business. Movie PIs rarely have money problems, but Gil had bills to pay and when clients didn't pay him, he filed in Small Claims. That day he had court date with a lawyer who wanted to chisel Gil on his bill. Gil had taken the case because the lawyer was an outside counsel for an insurance company, handling the defense in a case with elements of fraud. At first, the lawyer seemed to be a man of integrity, but Gil learned otherwise when he presented his bill. Gil knew the type. People like him used others to provide services as an interest-free source of operating capital, while having no intention of using someone's services more than once. Their credit reports ran to multiple pages and they would have trouble buying a washer and dryer on credit.

Gil dreaded the drive to the courthouse; the queue for the metal detectors, the obnoxious courthouse flunkies and the waste of time that could be better spent doing billable hours. Blessedly, the lawyer's secretary called with an offer of $1,800 to settle Gil's $2,500 bill. He knew that meant she had $2,000.

"Two thousand dollars and I pick up the check today."

She put Gil on hold. “Mr. Cairns said the check will be ready this afternoon,” she said after what seemed like a five-minute wait.

Now Gil would have his mortgage payment and some pocket money. He had learned over the years that people like Cairns weren’t worth the trouble of even one assignment. “Some of these guys would screw a snake if they could hold it down,” he had said more than once.

Privately, Gil had to consider how few resources were available to him. After all, Lieutenant Hara had all the resources of a modern police force. He could get search warrants. He had the forensics of fingerprinting, blood work and ballistics plus “feet on the street” to comb for witnesses and dig for informers. Gil had his 250-square-foot office, some photo and electronic equipment, a computer and little else.

He couldn’t dismiss this, but he would discount this mismatch for now. He knew he had to work smart if he was to get anywhere with David’s death. If Sabrina was right and David’s employers did have something to do with David’s death, then he had best look for a motive because a motive should point to a perpetrator.

He called Hara before he called Sabrina. Hara didn’t come to the phone. His clerk reported, “Lieutenant Hara says to tell you he’s not ignoring you. He just doesn’t have anything new on the Chang case.”

Gil reached Sabrina at her office at Lockard Aviation in Burbank. Even a cursory glance at the business pages would show that engineers like Sabrina designed spooky things for the Air Force, but they couldn’t discuss their work without risking fines or prison for disclosing classified information.

“Sabrina, I—we, if you want to help—can’t waste motion. If you’re right about your dad making mysterious calls, let’s see who he was calling. Grab your dad’s newest phone bills.”

“You got it, Uncle Gil. Anything else?”

"Look through your dad's home office. See if you can get a feel for what, if any, DaleeAhn Company records he may have had at home."

"Like what?"

"Don't know, because I don't know what I don't know yet. Your dad was an accountant—a stickler for detail. You said he was spending lots of time on his computer after hours. I've got to begin thinking he may have been involved in something."

"My dad? A crook?"

"It wouldn't have to be something illegal. As I said, I don't know what I don't know. Maybe he simply knew about something illegal. I don't think it's just coincidence he was spending so much time in his home office before his murder."

Sabrina became defensive. "Now he's a blackmailer?"

"Knowing your dad, not likely. But if he knew something that could have exposed someone to the law, to an employer, a wife, whatever—people have killed to prevent a spouse from learning about an affair. Doesn't have to be about money or something illegal."

"OK. Anything else?"

"I want to start looking into the formation and funding of DaleeAhn. It would really be nice to see the books, too. Remember that I did my time in corporate America among the marginally competent before going out on my own. Maybe we can find some clues along that avenue."

"Ooh, which reminds me. I almost forgot. When my dad, Ming and the other guy were setting up DaleeAhn, they used a consultant. Nice man—a Mr. Tillman. I think he lives in Diamond Bar."

"You mean with incorporation papers, setting up the books, that sort of thing?"

"Yes, he's some kind of retired executive and a CPA who does consulting. I think my dad took some courses in accounting from him at the community college."

"Thanks again. If I can't find his number in the book, I'll call you. Later, Sabrina."

Richard Heng called minutes before Gil left his office. "Mr. Rodrigues? This is Mr. Heng. We met after the funeral … "

Gil cut him off. "Of course, Mr. Heng. I've been waiting for your call."

They agreed to meet in an hour at a local Denny's 24-hour diner. Gil deliberately arrived early and selected a corner booth. Whatever Mr. Heng had to say was something he wanted to say without anyone listening. Gil asked the waitress to leave two menus because he was waiting for a second person. Just yards from the Pomona Freeway and a gas station, the diner served mostly people on their way to somewhere east of Los Angeles. Few locals ate here. It had been remodeled into a faux 50s look with glass blocks, stainless steel cabinetry and individual jukeboxes in the booths. On the walls were copies of Coca-Cola posters from about 1953. It wasn't as Gil remembered the time. The posters featured nubile, blond teenage girls in pleated skirts and saddle shoes. All wore ponytails. The girls in Gil's memory of high school had all looked liked nuns. The boys in the posters wore crew cuts or pompadours held in place with what looked like crankcase oil.

Heng approached Gil with the same deference he had shown him at the funeral luncheon. "Thank you for seeing me, Mr. Rodrigues."

Heng seated himself in the corner of the booth such that he could see the entire room. He placed a business card on the table in front of Gil. It read, "Richard Heng - Accounting and Bookkeeping." They ordered coffee. Gil was silent, allowing Heng to find his own comfort level before speaking.

Heng began. "Mr. Rodrigues, perhaps I should be speaking with the sheriff's people, but I have no experience with police activities. David spoke highly of you and I would feel better speaking with you first."

"I hope I merit your trust, Mr. Heng. Please tell me how I might help."

Heng took a breath and then swallowed visibly. "I know someone who might have had a reason to kill David."

Gil fought the impulse to speak. He had to let the man talk and not say anything that might inhibit him.

"Worse than that, I would feel considerable responsibility if my fears turned out to be true."

He paused, looked down at his tea and continued. "To understand, Mr. Rodrigues, you need to know that informal loans in the Asian communities for business purposes are very common. It's good for the borrower because he can't get a conventional loan from the bank, and it's good for the lender because he can make a good return in the short run."

"I think I know where this is going. You and David lent money to someone who had no intention of paying it back. When David threatened to talk to the law, he got himself killed."

"That is my fear. Since I am an accountant, clients will sometimes ask me for sources of short-term loans. They are prepared to offer large premiums."

"And you and David decided to make some side money?"

"This was only our second loan. We had pooled $35,000. Our first loan made us $1500 each in 30 days."

"That might be considered loan sharking or usury, you know. They'll both get one in trouble with the law."

Heng raised his finger to make his point instantly. "Except that there is no force or extortion here. Losing a loan may lose a friendship, too, but gets no one killed or injured."

"And with this second loan, you encountered some sort of a confidence man?"

"I'm not sure. That's my concern. When he failed to pay us back many weeks past the due date, David and I called on him. David threatened to speak with the authorities. The man became enraged and said only that we would be 'very regretful' if we went to the police."

"And why do you think this man might be capable of murder, Mr. Heng?"

"I can't be sure, but I can tell you I have never heard a more forceful threat. I just had a sense that the man was capable of anything."

"Has anyone besides you or David ever met this man?"

"No, not that I recall. Such persons like discretion in such matters. It can be embarrassing to be borrowing money in our culture."

"Do you know where he can be found?"

"I have the phone number he gave us at the time. It was a friend's number. He said his own phone number had not been installed yet."

"His name?"

"Mr. Yang. He adopted the name of Harold. I never knew his Chinese given name."

"Can you give me his number?"

Heng scribbled a phone number on the back of his own business card.

"What business did he say he was in?"

"He said he was importing consumer electronics from Singapore and Hong Kong."

"Where had you been meeting this man?"

"In restaurants like this. Much Chinese business is conducted in restaurants."

"So I understand, Mr. Heng." Gil paused. "Getting back to David, how did you come to know him?"

"We are both Buddhists. I met him at the weekly study group at the temple. Both of us were accountants and we came to this country about the same time and we live in the same area. We had much in common."

"And you went to the temple the night David was killed?"

Heng's eyes widened. "Why yes, but David never showed up."

"Are you aware David was seen in the parking lot that night, but as you said, he never showed up inside the temple?"

"I did not know that. I just assumed he couldn't come that night for some reason or another."

Both men looked into space for a few moments. Finally Gil spoke.

"Why haven't you gone directly to the sheriff's people with this information?"

"It's just suspicion and speculation on my part and I thought that you might give me some … " He hesitated.

Gil filled in. "Perspective or assessment?"

Heng seemed grateful for the word choice. "Yes, I fear I may be making too much of nothing. Also … " He hesitated.

Gil finished for him. "Also this money lending could be an embarrassment to his wife and friends. I understand." Gil paused and then looked straight at Heng. "I want you to call Detective Chin and tell him what you just told me. I have a legal and ethical obligation to report this, so I want you to report it first. I'll call Lieutenant Hara in a day or two to make sure you've passed this on."

Heng nodded yes and then murmured, "Yes, of course."

After they said their good-byes, Gil went back to his office. He called a man at a PI agency with whom he had been acquainted for a number of years. "Rudy, are you still doing asset and credit searches these days?"

"That's our stock in trade. Always has been. What's up?"

"I need a favor. Do me a credit check on a Richard Heng and Harold Yang. Heng uses his adopted name. I'm not sure about this Harold guy. If there's a charge, sue me." Gil read the address off Heng's business card. "If you can do both a personal and Dun and Bradstreet credit check that would be great and I'll owe you a beer—or I'll follow one of your many lady friends to see if she's cheating on you."

"Now that's something I might take you up on some time. Only take a couple of minutes. We're on line now, you know." There was a tone of pride in Rudy's voice.

"Can't deal with all this modern stuff, Rudy. I'm an 1800's guy trapped in a 1900's body. You should know that. Call me back."

"It should be easy with Heng," Rudy said, "given the address and business name. I might have trouble finding this Yang. Too common a name and nothing to narrow it down."

"Do the best you can, Rudy."

Rudy called back within fifteen minutes. "Gil, no luck with Yang. Too many around with that surname and Harold is likely an adopted name. But where did you meet this Heng?"

"He's a friend of a friend and it's a long story. What did you find out?"

"A printout of his credit reports would kill a few trees. The good news is that he's been in business for about ten years. The bad news is that this Heng owes everyone and his brother. There are some judgments against him, too. Judgments are death when it comes to credit ratings. He's got two equity mortgages on his house. On a scale of a thousand, this guy's credit is about a fifty."

"That bad, eh, Rudy?"

"That bad. You want a copy?"

"Fax it at your leisure, pal. I owe you a couple of pops. Thanks."

Gil dialed Yang's phone number. He got what he expected—an answering machine with a prerecorded greeting. He hung up.

Gil didn't want to call Hara quite yet about Heng. He didn't want to bias Hara's thinking toward the man in any way. Instead, he would wait until after Hara interviewed Heng. If Heng had invented this Harold Yang, then Heng would find himself a suspect in David's murder. This might turn out to be interesting.

CHAPTER SIX

Gil easily enough found Ron Tillman's phone number and home address in Diamond Bar, a city that lay at the eastern end of the San Gabriel Valley about forty miles east of Los Angeles. A bedroom community, Diamond Bar had a reputation for greater affluence than many of the older communities in Southern California. Some who study trends have said that its racial and ethnic mix was a template for California in the coming decades.

Whites, Chinese, Koreans, Japanese, Hispanics, Asian Indians and Middle Easterners in what demographers characterize as "professional-technical" occupations were typical of this city only about five miles from Cal Poly in Pomona. Small business owners, accountants, engineers, computer programmers, professors, teachers—name it and you'd find one or more in Diamond Bar along with the retired, who tended their gardens and played the golf course that occupied much of the city's northern border along the Orange Freeway. To census takers four of ten residents described themselves as "Asian."

Gil called Ron Tillman who picked up the phone. He could hear classical music playing in the background.

"Ron speaking."

"Mr. Tillman, I'm Gil Rodrigues. I knew David Chang. I understand you worked with David and his employers. Can we talk a little about them?'

"Are you with the Sheriff's Department?"

"Actually, I'm a private investigator." The statement was met with silence.

Gil held his breath. He knew Tillman would know that he had no obligation to speak with him. Gil added hastily, "It'll be off the record. Promise." Then he held his breath again for several beats.

He heard Tillman take a long sigh and then say, "OK. We have to go out tomorrow about mid-morning, but if you can get here before then I'll do what I can for you. I can't imagine how I can help you, but you're welcome to stop by for a bit. "

"Thanks, Ron. See you in the morning."

The Tillman home was in a neighborhood of two-story tract homes disguised so as not to look like tract homes. One was the mirror image of the other; one had a brick façade, another stucco. A well-tended yard and garden distinguished Tillman's home. It had barred windows and a "security" front door. Two video cameras scanned the driveway and sidewalk to the house.

Such security precautions were no longer unusual in California with its large numbers of immigrants, many of whom came from environments where such measures were a necessity. And Gil couldn't dismiss such precautions even though Diamond Bar had a miniscule crime rate. He guessed the Tillmans were in the twilight years and the town had been the site of one or two home-invasion robberies. This was a type of crime relatively rare until recently and visited almost exclusively on Asians by other Asians looking for money and valuables held in home safes hidden from the tax collector.

Gil rang the doorbell knowing that he could be seen on the monitor inside. Immediately, he heard one, and then two dogs barking. After what seemed like four or five minutes, a woman came to the door. Gil judged her to be in her early seventies and well preserved. She was a solid, midwestern type in blue jeans with gardener's gloves in hand. Her red hair, streaked with gray, was short in the style of older women and it was plain to Gil that she must have been strikingly beautiful as a young woman.

"I'm Joan Tillman. And you must be Mr. Rodrigues. Ron said you were coming."

The two dogs which Gil guessed to be of mixed breed burst out the door all the while barking at Gil and ignoring the woman's efforts to quiet them. "They don't bite," she assured Gil. "But they're good watch dogs."

Gil liked animals and never mistreated any, but the dogs continued barking such that one nearly had to shout over them.

"Handsome little fellows. Feisty, too," Gil managed with a forced smile.

Joan Tillman led Gil through a cluttered if tastefully decorated house to Tillman's office overlooking the golf course. "He's showering after his treadmill. Be out soon."

Gil sat in a chair half-facing Tillman's desk that was either oak or walnut and probably an antique. The desk was covered with files and on it sat a calculator, trailing about three feet of printed tape over the edge of the desk onto the floor. Law and tax books lined the walls along with photos of kids, pets, assorted diplomas, certificates and business awards.

The photo that caught Gil's attention, however, had been blown up to small poster size. It was a black and white in sharp focus of the crew of a B-29 standing under the nose art of the aircraft. It transfixed Gil and he stood and moved closer to it. Ron Tillman was Major Tillman back then and he couldn't have been more than twenty-two or twenty-three. Among other decorations, he had been awarded the Distinguished Flying Cross, not once, but twice. They hung in a frame next to the photo.

Gil was still studying the picture when heard Tillman's voice behind him. "Hard to believe we were ever that young."

Gil gave only a quick glance at Tillman and continued to study the faces of these young men over four decades ago on some island he guessed was Guam. "I think we all have the same thought when we look at these pictures," Gil said. "Maybe it was some parallel life and these pictures are here to taunt us."

Tillman and Gil faced each other. Tillman was wearing a sweat suit. His hair, nearly silver, was still damp from the shower. He stood at eye level with Gil. That made him over six feet. "You sound like a mystic—or at least somebody thoughtful."

"Mystic?" Gil laughed. "Me? No, not likely. Probably speaks more to alarm over the aging process. Don't know if I've ever been quite that spiritual. I leave that to guys like David and their friends with the saffron robes and sandals."

"About my same thoughts, Mr. Rodrigues. I've looked at that picture every day to remind me that I'm the only survivor of my squadron. Yes, sir, wars are for the young to fight and die in, Mr. Rodrigues."

"Call me Gil."

"Call me Ron." They shook hands.

Gil's interest in the photo got Tillman talking. "I was discharged from the Army Air Force on my twenty-third birthday in '45. I had led one of the largest bomb raids of the war. My best friend got it when his plane took a direct hit on the bomb load."

Tillman caught himself before showing any more emotion.

"We all have our ghosts, Ron."

"You seem a little young for the Second."

"Yes, by about fifteen years or so. They sent us to Vietnam in '61. 'Civilian Technical Advisors' they called us at first, but eventually they dropped that b.s. and made us put the uniforms back on."

"Nasty place, Indochina, but you didn't come here to swap war stories."

Joan Tillman burst into the room without so much as an "excuse me," the two dogs at her heels barking at Gil again. He tried to pet them, but they danced away.

"Ron, don't forget we promised the Goughs we'd be there on time," Joan reminded her husband.

"We'll make it, dear." It was the "dear" of a lifetime together. "I have to finish with Gil, here. Take the dogs, please."

Gil sat through this interruption with the half-smile one wears for bratty kids or annoying pets. Blessedly, she left with the dogs.

"Not sure if I can help you, Gil, but I'll try. You think these guys at DaleeAhn had something to do with David's murder?"

"His daughter does, but she dislikes them. As for me, right now I just don't know. It still looks like a street crime, quite frankly. How'd you get hooked up with these guys, Ron?"

"Met David in an accounting class I taught for a while at the junior college. David never became a CPA and referred clients to me who needed help in setting up, buying or selling a business. Last direct contact I had with David was about two months ago."

"And?"

"He asked me for some accounting advice and bitched a little."

"About?"

"He was never real specific, but he didn't like the principals at DaleeAhn. 'Bad people, bad people,' he'd say, but he wouldn't elaborate and, frankly, I didn't press. Didn't want to get involved."

"You helped these guys set up the DaleeAhn Corporation?"

"It's easy money. Helped them draw up the incorporation papers, find office space, set up the books and just generally help them get started. Imagine you and I going to China and trying to set up a business. We'd need local help."

"That was your only involvement?"

"Yes, and I made it my last one. Can't give you a solid answer why."

"You didn't like these guys, either, did you?"

"Couldn't put my finger on it. They just didn't seem to be who they said they were. I asked about where they wanted to go with DaleeAhn and they'd give me vague answers about importing Chinese products and exporting American products, but I didn't see any of that while I was there."

"Where does the money come from?"

"Their m.o. is to set up a U.S. corporation or buy an existing American business. Then they create a joint venture with a Chinese company that invests capital in the American company."

"So far nothing wrong," Gil said.

"Correct. Even after a main bank in China wire transfers some big bucks into the corporate account to fund it all. Hundreds of these JV's around the country."

"How much in the way of funding?"

"Five million. I was still there to make the accounting entry."

"Five mill? Must have been one helluva business plan."

"I never saw a business plan if there was one. I offered to write one—for a fee, of course. Maybe there's one in China somewhere. They told you what they wanted you to know whether it was true or not."

"So it must have been a done deal before they came here."

"You're the investigator, not me. Go figure. Ever try to get ten cents, much less five mill out of a venture capital outfit or a bank when you have no history?"

"No, but I hear it's a bitch. When did the disenchantment set in, Ron?"

"Accumulation of things. They immediately bought two Mercedes with company funds, and—ready for this?—registered them in their own names and then had the company pick up the tab on the insurance and maintenance."

"Ouch!" Gil said. "That'll get an auditor's attention."

"You bet. And David was stuck with his old Honda," Tillman added.

"Then they drove them like demolition derby?"

"How'd you guess, Gil? Then there were the dinner parties and trips to Vegas. They dragged my wife and me to one of the dinners. Spared no expense. They'd sit and talk Chinese to each other as if you weren't there then switch to English when it suited them."

"Did they ever give you a clue as to their backgrounds?"

"Not much. Part of my charter was to put resumes together for the principals. Ming, maybe the other one, too, went to some—I think—Beijing College of International Relations or some such. And one of their guests—forgot his name—was a merchant marine officer and a mean little bastard, too, but not officially part of the business. They seemed to know him from China."

"'Mean,' you say?"

"Did you ever see that news item in the *Times* a while back? Officers on a Chinese merchant ship threw three Czech stowaways overboard on the high seas?"

Gil's eyes widened. "It made the evening news, too. Other crew members got so scared they ran to the harbor authorities when the ship docked in Long Beach."

"Well, they were drunk as skunks and were talking in Chinese as usual and laughing. I mean like they were going to blow a gasket so they had to tell us what was so funny. Turned out they were laughing at that story and doing pantomime throwing gestures. I never did ask if this guy had been one of the ship's officers."

"About as funny as cancer. Ever meet any of their pals or associates?"

"They had some smooth, diplomatic type from the Chinese consulate at one party. He would drop into the office now and then to cadge a lunch or dinner. And the two were always on the phone with the door closed."

"You think he had a role in the business?" Gil asked.

"I had a sense that this consulate guy had some oversight role, but I can't be sure. None of them had been in the States all that long, but they seemed to know a lot of people here already."

"Why do think David was so unhappy?"

"Don't know for sure. They certainly treated him like dirt. Trivial errands, studied rudeness—that sort of thing. Seemed like some sort of class thing. And David hated the high living and pissing away company money so they must have picked up on that, too."

"Did they ever try to get you back?"

"Ming called me a couple of times asking 'hypothetical' questions about acquiring other companies. When I asked him if he had any company in mind and he said something to the effect of owning companies to export 'modern'—the word he used—products to China."

"'Modern', as in high-tech?"

"Didn't ask. By then I was tired of these guys. I lied. Told him I was retired. Fact is, I did my due diligence in setting up the books, etc. The place was clean when I left. Wasn't going to hang around until someone in China hired an American CPA firm to do an audit to find out how these guys were pissing away money."

Tillman was getting restless and stood up. "Don't want be rude, Gil, but I have to think about getting ready to go out with Joan."

"I can't thank you enough for seeing me, Ron."

"I can only hope it helps." Gil's respect for Tillman and members of his generation bordered on reverence. He wanted to tell Tillman that it was an honor to meet him, but he knew that that would embarrass him. They shook hands. The dogs barked at Gil again all the way out.

Gil stopped at his office to check his mail, his answer machine and to use the phone.

Sam Woo taught math in the high school Gil's kids had attended. Woo had been educated in Hong Kong and was probably overqualified for his job, but that hadn't hurt the kids. Gil phoned Sam at his home.

"Sam—I hope I've got this right." Gil slowed his speech. "The Beijing College of International Relations? What do you know about it?"

"Where'd you pick that up, Gil?"

"Is there such a place?"

"There sure is. Where I come from it is common knowledge that the College of International Relations in Beijing is run by the MSS—Ministry of State Security." He paused. "The MSS is sort of a Chinese version of the CIA and FBI combined. Their spies and diplomats go there."

Gil said nothing.

"Gil ... you still there?"

"I'm here, Sam." Gil had to catch himself. He was almost stammering. "Thanks, Sam. Thanks a bunch. Gotta run."

Back in his car, Gil found himself mumbling to himself. He spoke the words slowly and out loud. "The Beijing College of International Relations. Sure doesn't sound like a community college." He was now eager to meet the officers of the DaleeAhn Corporation once again.

CHAPTER SEVEN

On the way to an interview for one of his fraud cases, Gil passed the elementary school where David had served as a volunteer tutor and reader. It made Gil smile to remember David's attempts to recruit him as a tutor. His efforts had been a waste because Gil knew he didn't have the temperament or desire to be helping kids with their schoolwork. Even older kids got on his nerves with their empty-headed stares and lack of interest in anything that required study or reading. "No," he thought, "we could thank our stars for people like David." And, he knew such people had to include his late wife, who clearly enjoyed teaching the young.

He drove to an address in Azusa on Foothill Boulevard—what "historic" Route 66 is called in this part of California—where he interviewed a doctor involved in an injury case, after which he returned to his office. There he finished his report of the interview and then headed home where he made himself a drink and turned on the six o'clock news. Earlier, on the car radio, he had heard some "headline" news to the effect that several experts were predicting the largest stock market crash in decades. The lead story on the TV news at six, however, dealt with the fatal shooting of the Korean owner of a convenience store in Los Angeles. It had all been caught on tape by the store's security cameras, making the news director's selection of a lead story for that day an easy matter. They played and replayed the victim's dance of death that began when the bullet entered his body. Maybe the news at seven would deal with a replay of The Crash of '29.

Gil was hungry, but felt too lazy to cook and too lazy to eat out. He would do what he did on so many other nights—open a can of "chunky" soup and wash it down with a Merlot he bought in three-liter bottles. He continued to sift through his conversation with Ron Tillman, searching for some nuggets in the sand. And Sam Woo's description of Ming's alma mater as a spy school got him to thinking way beyond David's murder.

In itself, that Ming or anyone else might have trained and worked as a spook was neither noteworthy nor cause for alarm. In the U.S. alone there had to be thousands of former spooks from just the Cold War and Vietnam era. Gil himself received an occasional newsletter from an association of former intelligence people in Virginia.

The world was full of former members of security and intelligence agencies. Like Arthur Miller salesmen who greet the world with a smile and a shoeshine, they're a dime a dozen. Having acquired in early adulthood a competence more suitable for warfare or spying didn't make one a bad person, bad citizen, bad parent or bad businessman, and it didn't make one a murderer, either. On the other hand, if Ming was in the U.S. on a mission from Chinese intelligence in Beijing, then Gil might be in over his head even more than he thought when he stepped into this.

For his self-preservation, however, Gil had to have a Plan B to cover himself with the feds if it should turn out that DaleeAhn was a cover for some kind of MSS operation. Right now, he had nothing but suspicions, and to bring suspicions to the feds at this point would be premature. Worse, it might make him look like some nut or attention-seeker. There was no benefit to reporting suspicions and weakening his credibility, if he could find hard evidence later on.

It was labeled "beef," but the soup seemed to contain mostly potatoes and salt. The salt content made Gil pucker and the jug wine didn't do much to improve this meal even after he splashed a tablespoon of it into the bowl. He pushed it aside unfinished and nibbled on some saltines. *"If Helen saw the junk I was eating, she'd ... "* He quickly pushed the thought of her aside. If he was going to find David's killer he had to work smarter than he ever had before. He tried to focus on the basics: motive, opportunity, and means. The books say that if you answer those basics, then you should find your killer. Speculation wouldn't help. Gil needed evidence, but wasn't sure where to go next.

The phone rang. It was Sabrina. She seemed excited. "That Detective Chin called me. They feel pretty strongly about a carjacker they've identified and are looking to arrest. The victims described a small caliber handgun."

"That's encouraging, honey. How did he leave it with you?"

"They don't have prints, but I suppose he could have worn gloves. He does have a history of carjacking Hondas."

"Yes, honey. They're popular with car thieves. Let's hope they're on to something."

"Any news on your end, Unc?"

"I met with Tillman today. He confirmed what you already told me."

"Which is?"

"That your dad's erstwhile employers are assholes, probably thieves, and maybe some kind of spies into the bargain."

"Is that all? Well, I suppose that's progress."

"Did these guys ever show any interest in your work at Lockard?"

"Not outright. The one time I got dragged to one of their awful dinner parties, Ming asked me something about whether Lockard ever considered sending any of their employees to science conferences or seminars outside the U.S."

"Like mainland China?"

"That was my sense, but I said no just to blow it off. If I wanted to visit China, I'd do it on my own ticket, not with that jerk sneaking looks at my ass or sitting in conferences with a bunch of engineering nerds."

"Subject ever come up again?"

"I think he tried through my dad, but my dad seemed to feel the same and that was the last time it ever came up. Why do you ask?"

"Just a thought, Sabrina. Just a thought."

"You think we'll ever learn who did it?"

"Frankly, and if I had to bet, I'd say not without a break of some sort. Somehow, I don't think your dad's murder was an impulse. I think your dad's murder was set up and carried out by a person or persons who knew just how to do it so as to get away with it. No fingerprints, witnesses, et cetera—so far at least."

"You mean like a hired killer?"

"Hara and I kicked that one around. Maybe not in the Mafia sense, but someone who knew how to kill someone even in a crowd and walk away clean."

"You know about those things, don't you, Uncle Gil?"

"I read a lot. Any luck with your dad's records?"

"Yes. I'm no accountant, but it looks like he kept lots of company records on his computer. Maybe they're duplicates of what he had at his work. I don't know. I should have the phone bill tomorrow."

"Let's look them over ASAP. I'm hoping they'll point us somewhere. 'Bye, honey."

"Oh—Uncle Gil. I nearly forgot. Ming called about dropping off Dad's personal things from the office."

"Great! Tell him to hold on to them. Tell him I expect to be in the area and offered to pick them up."

Gil was pleased at the news. Volunteering to pick up David's personal effects relieved Gil of having to manufacture a pretext to visit the offices where David had worked.

Gil's thoughts shifted to Heng. His story about making a bad loan together with David was troubling Gil. And, it was time to suck up to Hara a bit by reminding him how well he was heeding his advice to pass on important information. He called Hara. "Did Richard Heng get in touch with you, Steve?"

"Yes, he did." Hara sounded pleased. "He told us that you insisted he tell us about his and David's loan to Harold Yang."

"Just doing what you told me, Steve."

"Yeah, right. Like you always do."

"I checked Heng's credit," Gil said. "He doesn't have a pot to pee in. He'd have plenty of motives for scamming someone like David and then having him killed if he complained. Frankly, I doubt if he put up two nickels for a loan to anyone. The bigger question I have is whether this Yang even exists. That's why I insisted he tell his story to you."

"I would have had the same suspicion if we didn't have other complaints against this Yang," Hara said. No, he's real and we know how to find him, but he's been hard to nail."

"Why so, Steve?"

"The DA doesn't have many people assigned to white-collar crime, so he goes after the clear-cut fraud cases where the convictions are easy."

"Gotcha. White-collar crime is hard to prosecute anyway, I imagine. It requires some brains, too. Stick with car theft and drug possession. Easy stuff."

Gil's sarcasm wasn't lost on Hara, who just had to find an object lesson here. "But you did the right thing in sending him to us."

"I'll throw you a Boy Scout salute next time I see you."

Hara groaned. "Forever the wise ass, aren't you, Gil? I don't know why I put up with you."

"I don't know, either, Steve, but thanks for doing so." Gil's thoughts were already turned toward tomorrow and his chance to meet David's bosses again and to reconnoiter the offices where David had worked.

CHAPTER EIGHT

Gil headed for the DaleeAhn Corporation in City of Industry, in the heart of the San Gabriel Valley where he had practiced his profession and raised a family. He took the Pomona Freeway west at the tail end of the morning rush hour and surrendered to his inclination to become contemplative in the slow traffic.

Tourist books say that this valley is named for a Spanish mission of that same name in what became the city of San Gabriel. That mission is one of twenty-one constructed and consecrated over two centuries ago along *El Camino Real*—The Royal Road. Those missions were supposed to bring Christianity and an enlightened life to the heathen natives. The reality was that men lured to California by tales of gold and land enlightened no one. Instead of enlightening the heathens, they drove them to extinction through overwork, disease and the lash. To Gil, that record meant that even this slice of suburbia had been paid for in blood.

Points of interest and entertainment in the San Gabriel Valley include the Rose Bowl, the Norton Simon Museum, Caltech and the Jet Propulsion Lab, all at the western end of Pasadena, a city some regard as not part of this formless valley. Large areas of the valley, overrun by immigrants—both legal and illegal, and mostly from Mexico, China, Korea and India—have taken on a blight and scramble for personal space, making many neighborhoods in the valley resemble nothing so much as a third-world country.

The DaleeAhn Corporation occupied a one-story, concrete-slab building. Such buildings exist in the thousands in industrial parks throughout California. Typically, each offers about 1000 square feet of floor space. The office space sits in the front of the building. The rear of the building houses inventory or manufacturing, shipping and receiving.

Gil estimated there were fifteen such buildings in the U-shaped complex. All seemed to be occupied. Some had signs in English and Chinese; some in English only; some in Chinese only. Gil didn't count, but he estimated that half of the cars parked in the common lot were late-model Mercedes or BMWs, cars of choice for immigrants who have "arrived."

There was no reception area at DaleeAhn. When Gil opened the door, he stepped directly into an office area with three desks. The bare one must have been David's.

Ming and Liao sat at the other two. Ming sat at his desk behind a glass partition. The office air was nearly gray with cigarette smoke, the smell of which seemed to be mixed with the odor of garlic.

Except for the colors—mostly tan—the furniture reminded Gil of a government office. The desks were of plain metal as were the filing cabinets; the chairs were a mix of clerical and "executive" styles. The fabrics didn't match at all. It was obvious that that most of the furniture had been bought used. Most surfaces were covered with dust, the windows hadn't been washed in months, and each ashtray held dozens of cigarette butts. There was little paperwork visible on the desks. A small kitchen nook held a sink and a microwave, both of which were splattered with food.

Liao and Ming both left their chairs at nearly the same moment.

Ming offered his hand. "Mr. Rodrigues, how good of you to come for David's things. I hope you were not inconvenienced. Mr. Liao would have delivered them."

"No, I have some business in the area."

"And how has David's family been bearing up?"

"About as well as can be expected."

Ming was at his smarmy best. "We Chinese have a proverb, 'There is no grief greater than for a dead heart.'"

"And my dad liked to say, 'Great grief is mute.'"

"I see you, too, are wise in this emotion, Mr. Rodrigues. Let us go to our little conference room. Would you like a cup of tea?"

"That sounds good. Plain is fine."

Liao motioned Gil towards the conference room. Gil smiled and made an after-you stage gesture so as to follow the two men. Gil knew what to look for in a quick a sweep of the room. He normally billed clients an hourly rate for three hours to perform a security survey, with recommendations, for a building this size. He saw no alarm decals in the front window, no motion detectors, no visible video cameras, no wire leads to doors or windows, and no control box to indicate a burglar alarm. The front door had a single barrel lock. And with no burglar alarm, there were unlikely to be hidden video cameras.

Gil saw only two file cabinets, the locks of which were painted over. The desks had locks, but he knew that desks bought used are often missing their keys. Computers were different. They might have locks or password protection. No way to tell without a closer look.

What really caught Gil's eye was the key rack on the wall next to the door of the washroom. And the keys had tags that he hoped were printed in English.

None of this apparent lack of security surprised Gil. Of all people, Ming and Liao would know that locks and keys or alarms wouldn't protect them against a search under warrant if it ever came to that. If they were doing anything illegal, they knew that their best protection was to keep a low profile among the thousands of Asians in Southern California and to maintain an outward appearance of being legitimate businessmen.

Liao brought in three stained ceramic cups containing hot water and placed them on the conference table. Ming and Liao scooped some loose green tea into their cups. They handed Gil a tea bag.

On the conference table was a cardboard box. "Mr. Liao put David's personal items into this box," Ming said, touching the box lightly. "If you would like to inspect … "

"No need for that, Mr. Ming. I'll bring them to Mei Chang this afternoon."

"We will have difficulty replacing David. He was very capable. If you know anyone, Mr. Rodrigues, we would be grateful. We place great value on personal recommendations."

"I'll keep that in mind. You know, I never knew exactly what kind of business David was in. What is it you folks do here?"

"We came here and formed a joint venture with a Chinese company on the mainland. We try to find American products we might sell in China and Chinese products we might sell in America. It is—as you Americans like to say—a 'challenge'!"

Gil smiled at the comment. "Yes, a 'challenge'. It helps us make believe those jobs we hate are really very stimulating and gratifying. Any products I might recognize?"

"You are a businessman yourself, Mr. Rodrigues?"

The half-smirk on Ming's face meant he knew the answer already, as would any competent cross-examiner who never asks a question without knowing the answer.

"I worked in the corporate world for a number of years. I've been self-employed as an insurance investigator now for awhile."

"It must be interesting work, Mr. Rodrigues, but to answer your question, we seek products and technologies to help bring China into the modern world. Items commonplace in your country are sometimes rare or nonexistent in China."

"Yes, we're blessed in that way. We have plenty of things."

Ming flashed a smile. "If it's not too personal of me, you seem to have a certain—*bearing*—Mr. Rodrigues. Were you ever a military man or athlete?"

"Both—for a while when I was young."

"We are of the same generation, so I can understand," Ming said.

Gil changed the subject. "I'd guess your search for products includes things more complicated than blenders and hair dryers."

Ming slapped the tabletop. "You have a wonderful sense of humor, Mr. Rodrigues." Liao looked puzzled until Ming translated and they laughed politely.

The meeting was a charade, but it was accomplishing Gil's purpose so far. It was a just a reconnaissance exercise.

Gil started to rise. "I must be on my way. Thanks for taking care of David's things and thank you for the tea. May I use your washroom?"

"Of course, Mr. Rodrigues." Ming pointed the way.

"I'll be back for the box in a moment." It was the right move; they would wait for him to come back to the conference room.

Gil opened the door to the washroom and turned on the light, after taking a fast glance over his shoulder at the key rack. One key was labeled "Warehouse." Gil dropped it into his pocket, entered the washroom and closed the door. He waited a few moments, then flushed the toilet and washed his hands. He rejoined Ming and Liao before taking his good-byes with the box in hand.

Gil drove back to his office, but he needed to stop at the market first. He had more to do at DaleeAhn before he went home for the evening.

CHAPTER NINE

Gil could go to jail for breaking and entering, burglary, or both. If caught, at a minimum, he would lose his license, but if he played Hamlet thinking too much on the deed, then he wouldn't do it at all. It would be nice if Hara had probable cause for a search warrant, but he didn't. Instead, Gil was operating on the presumption that either or both of the two officers of the DaleeAhn Corporation were involved in David's murder, but that presumption might be dead wrong. Gil would mention his plans for this evening to no one. To do so might make someone Gil loved subject to prosecution as an accessory if he got caught. Taking risks can make one a winner. It can also make one a loser.

At the food market, Gil found latex gloves in the aisle with cleaning products. Then, back in his office, he grabbed some blank computer disks. The pocket flashlight was in his car. He would wear a blazer, as he always did when on business. Only a nitwit would play the Ninja; there was no need to call unnecessary attention to himself.

He parked across the street, but at an angle that allowed him to watch the front door of DaleeAhn through his rear-view mirror. He wore a baseball cap to break the contour of his head from the rear. It was 4:45 P.M. He was gambling that all of the tenants in the complex did not shut their doors promptly at five. He didn't want to call attention to himself as the sole person in the area; the trick was to look like you belonged there. At 5:10, the two men who represented DaleeAhn emerged from the front door and left in their Mercedes.

Gil waited ten minutes and then drove to the access area behind the complex. Facing the complex was the windowless rear wall of another complex. His luck was holding. In the rear of the building was a roll-up freight door as well as a door for pedestrians. Gil parked head on to the roll-up door. Several doors down he could see someone loading a van with some boxes. There were three vehicles in sight and each represented a potential witness.

Gil pulled on the latex gloves and then left his car. He walked briskly to the door for pedestrians, took a quick look right and left and tried the key. It fit, but hadn't been used much. Both lock and key were nearly new; Ming must have had the locks changed when he moved in. After several twists, Gil got the door open. He took another quick look left and right and then entered the building, without letting the door slam behind him.

This warehouse portion of the building was windowless. It would have been nearly pitch black except for some late afternoon sunlight from an open door to the office area. On the remote chance that someone was still in the building, Gil stood perfectly still. He had considered the possibility of bumping into a night janitor, but the dust and mess in the washroom told him that was unlikely. And he had to consider the possibility that DaleeAhn had a zone-type burglar alarm for the rear of the building only.

Moving slowing, he did a sweep with his flashlight for motion detectors. If he spotted one, then, for his safety, he would assume it had triggered an intrusion alert at an alarm company, which would dispatch its own patrol or call the local police. In that case, Gil would walk, not run, to his car, drive away slowly and hope to be gone before anyone arrived. Just the thought made his heart race even though he had managed to stay relatively calm until then.

He had to believe that the adrenaline rush was part of a burglar's motivation, but burglary was no way he would ever make a living. For an instant Gil had to fight the impulse to leave. The first effect of adrenaline was one of nausea, not excitement. He reminded himself that when he lived in the body of a younger man he had had more balls than brains. This had allowed him to lurk sometimes within yards of the enemy; miles from his own camp, and with only a sidearm to blow his own brains out to avoid capture. At that time, capture meant torture and possibly even death somewhere in Hanoi; his two-bit burglary would mean humiliation and possibly jail. That threat scared him more than the ones of his youth. He chided himself: "Rodrigues, you've become too much of a pussy for this stuff. Get on with it and get out of here before you pee your pants."

Gil had been in the building for less than a minute. As his eyes adjusted to the dim light, he began looking about the warehouse, largely empty except for two large pieces of equipment and some smaller boxes sitting on pallets only a few feet from the freight door. He moved closer to them. Their weight had to be measured in tons and their cost in six-digits. He brought his flashlight to bear. Whatever they were, they were brand new and strapped to oversized pallets. They smelled of grease and paint. Gil shined his light on the packing and shipping documents. They seemed to be nearly identical. Each had some sort of computerized control unit with a video screen and keypad printed with a manufacturer's logo and the letters "CNC." Their documents revealed the shipper to be a machine tool distributor in southern California. The item descriptions read, "Machining Center—CNC—Six-Axis." The ID plates were stamped with "Graybill Machine Tool Co. Cleveland, Ohio." The documents on some smaller boxes described the contents as "cutting tools - diamond-tipped." The destination was listed only as a freight forwarder at the Port of Los Angeles. Gil wrote down the names, addresses and phone numbers of the freight forwarder and distributor.

The shipping documents on the smaller boxes described the contents as "Diagnostic Testing Kits—Hepatitis." They had been purchased from a medical supplies distributor. Here too, the destination was listed only as the same freight forwarder.

One item on the documents made him blink. DaleeAhn had paid for them C.O.D. That meant that someone at DaleeAhn had presented either a certified check or cash for this equipment when it had been delivered. Gil knew something of capital equipment sales. None but a very large company—or someone who wanted to mask the location and ownership and to avoid a security interest in the equipment—would buy anything of this nature with cash. A leasing company or mortgage holder would need to know the location of this equipment at all times.

Now came the riskier part of Gil's foray. He had to enter the office section of the premises. He had considered breaking into the building later in the evening, but that would mean searching the office entirely by flashlight, and that would enhance his chances of being spotted by someone who might dial 911.

It was still daylight and Gil had been inside less than five minutes. He walked to the door of the offices, stopped and listened; he heard nothing. Slowly he opened the door a crack to let his eyes adjust. The blinds were at a half-tilt. That meant someone walking by might see him. He would have to work fast and move about as if he belonged there. That meant sitting as much as possible.

His first stop was Ming's office. He sat down. The trick was to look but leave everything where he found it. He opened the desk's file drawer. The first file that caught Gil's attention contained newspaper and trade clippings. He placed it on the desk and thumbed through it. It contained stuff generated by press releases—new product announcements, contract awards, mergers. Ming wasn't stupid; he had collected all these clippings for some reason. Gil looked for a common thread. He found it among the phrases circled or highlighted—phrases such as "defense contract," "satellite," and "communications technology."

About midway in the pile was a news item about Lockard Aviation from the Business Section of the *Los Angeles Times*. Some references to "stealth technology" and "composites" were circled, but what really caught Gil's attention was handwriting at the top of the clipping. It read only, "Sabrina?" The question mark as punctuation intrigued Gil as much as the notation of Sabrina's name.

Gil thumbed through the rest of the stack, but it seemed to be more of the same. He carefully put the file back into the drawer. The other files contained correspondence. Some were faxes in Chinese. Gil considered copying them on the office copy machine, but he quickly dismissed that thought. To decipher them, he would have to hire a translator and that meant some stranger could guess that Gil had stolen the documents. He couldn't take that chance. Nor would he compromise Sabrina, her mother or Diana by asking them to translate.

And, if Ming were, in fact, working under orders from the MSS, he and his bosses would know that such traffic might be monitored by U.S. intelligence. That fact alone meant there would be little of importance in these faxes.

The other files contained letters from Ming on DaleeAhn letterhead. Most were addressed to companies in the clipping file. "We at DaleeAhn are desirous of meeting with your representatives at some mutually convenient time for the purpose of discussing the feasibility of a business relationship between our two companies such that might allow us to import your products into Asia." Some had responses attached, most of which referred Ming to representative of their Asian markets in Hong Kong, Taiwan or Australia. Others welcomed the inquiry.

Gil heard footsteps outside and froze. The footsteps faded and he heard a car door close and the car drive off, but it had been enough of a scare to give him a chill.

He couldn't possibly look at every file; he would have to sample them. He opened a file cabinet drawer labeled "Purchase Orders - A-D." All were cut for big-ticket, high-tech items such as machine tools, electronics equipment, computers, computer-assisted design software and microprocessors. Payment terms were all C.O.D. and the destination was always the same freight forwarder in the Port of Los Angeles.

Gil nearly slammed the drawer shut, but caught himself. He made sure everything was as he had found it. He would not try to copy files to the disks he had brought along. Looking through and then copying computer files would take too long and increase his chances of getting caught. He had seen enough for the time being. He returned the key to the key rack and slipped out the back door as quietly as he had entered. He put the latex gloves in his pocket. More than one burglar had been caught when the police found his fingerprints on the inside of a pair of latex gloves.

The next morning Gil checked the Yellow Pages for machine tool distributors and found several within a thirty-minute drive of his home. He phoned the one with the biggest ad, which read "since 1947" and asked for the sales manager. A Greg Williams picked up.

"Mr. Williams, I'm Gil Rodrigues, a freelance business writer. I need a basic tutorial in machine tools for a story I'm doing on manufacturing. I can promise a plug for your business when I do the piece. Can you help me? I have a deadline coming up in two days."

Williams was accommodating. "We do demos in our showroom almost daily. I believe we have some prospects coming this afternoon about two. I don't see any harm in your standing in quietly as an observer. You can just act as if you're part of the staff if you like or I'd be happy to introduce you as a trade reporter."

Gil picked up a reporter's notebook at in a stationery store in order to look the part. He liked the fact that the cover actually said, "Reporter's Notebook." At the distributor's shop, he stood several feet behind four men who were shopping for an additional machine tool. The demonstration was fascinating. The salesman explained how Computerized Numerical Control—CNC—software controlled a machine that sliced and diced a block of stainless steel into an incredibly complex valve with multiple ports, each of which was of a different diameter.

Gil played the role by taking notes. Afterward, he managed to buttonhole a member of Williams's staff for some additional questions. The young man introduced himself as Art and seemed to be flattered to be interviewed by a reporter.

"You must sell lots of these to the defense industry," Gil said.

"At least eighty percent of our business comes from the defense industry here in Southern California," Art said. "So you can imagine the millions of precision parts that go into aircraft and ships and weapons."

"Yes, it's fascinating." The conviction in Gil's voice was real. "I imagine countries like China would like to get their hands on gadgets like these."

Art raised his eyebrows. "You bet. They have machine tools, of course, but our stuff here is state-of-the-art, so we have to stay alert when foreign buyers come around so we don't get into trouble with U.S. Customs."

"How could you get into trouble?" Gil asked.

Art's tone became patronizing. "That should be obvious. You need a license to export these to some countries."

"Oh, of course," Gil said. "I should have known. Thanks so much for the demo."

Gil didn't want to show any more interest in the export issue to the salesman, but it had piqued his curiosity and he would explore it further. He didn't have to be a manufacturing engineer to know that the items sitting at DaleeAhn awaiting pick-up weren't hardware store gadgets. They were precision machines—very complex, very expensive, and not designed and built to make hubcaps, pots or pans.

CHAPTER TEN

Gil got up at six, went for his jog and did his light workout with weights. When he got to his office he found a fax from Koenig with a two new assignments. One case involved a medical clinic in Monterey Park. The second involved a suspicious rash of job-stress claims from recently laid-off workers, all of whom shared the same lawyer and doctor.

Gil would make a trip to Monterey Park and the medical clinic. He would deal with the job job-stress matter on another day.

First, however, he called a customs broker he picked at random out of the Yellow Pages. The sales manager's comments about Customs were nagging Gil and wanted to put a finer edge on those comments.

He asked the receptionist to speak with a customs broker.

"This is Lisa Snider. How can I help?"

"Morning, Lisa! My name's Rick Saint John. I'm a manufacturer's rep for several machine tool makers. I've been talking to a prospect. Said he wants to buy and ship to China. I don't have a deal yet, but figured I'd better talk to someone like you. Not sure what I need to know about the paperwork. Don't have any experience with export."

The broker gave Gil what seemed like a stock answer. "Mr. Saint John, we're always happy to take on new clients, but I can't give you a course in export law on the phone. I try to keep my clients out of trouble with U.S. Customs laws. They can be complicated and we're here to help you, but you have to be careful or you can wind up with a federal rap if you ship something prohibited for export. We can help get an export license if it's necessary. We have some guidelines I could send you with my business card. "

"Federal rap? Wow!" Gil hoped he wasn't over-acting. "Maybe I can crib some of your stuff into my proposal to cover my tail."

"That's what most of my clients do. The whole idea of these regs is to keep certain items out of the hands of bad guys. You may need an export license for China."

"But I sell machine tools."

"A machine tool can be used to make, say, gears for a truck transmission. Nothing wrong with that, but with the right software, someone in China or Iraq might be able to cut parts for a missile or submarine. Our Customs people call that a 'dual-purpose' item."

"I see. That's the stuff I'd have to watch. Guess I need to be careful, Lisa. Could you send me your booklet with your business card?" Gil gave her a phony address.

Tourists headed for the original Chinatown in Los Angeles were in for a disappointment. Tour bus operators stopped there only by special request. This twenty-five-block district was about a half-mile east of LA's Civic Center and downtown business district. It had been a bustling place until the mid-seventies when the population shift of Chinese immigrants east into the San Gabriel Valley and its cities like Monterey Park changed all that.

Now that there were a lot of closed stores in LA's Chinatown, the low rents attracted non-Asian artists and fashion designers who opened galleries, a fact that never sat well with Chinese preservationists. That same shift had created a number of smaller Chinatowns east of LA. Typically they consisted of a strip or mini-mall where Chinese owned most, and sometimes all, of the businesses. That day, Gil's business would bring him to one such Chinese strip mall in Monterey Park, about ten miles east of East Los Angeles.

Gil was back to earning a living—at least for one day. He dressed in a faded Lakers tee shirt, worn slacks and scruffy running shoes. He would drop in on a storefront medical clinic in Monterey Park.

The signs in the window were in English, Spanish and Chinese. The window was filled with stick-on vinyl signs: "Español Dichos," "Massage," "Chiropractic," "Acupuncture," "Herbs," "We accept most medical insurance."

There were two female receptionists; one was Asian, the other Hispanic. People in the waiting room were speaking English, Spanish and Mandarin. The Hispanic woman addressed Gil. "Yes, sir?"

"My lawyer sent me here. I was in a car accident."

She gave Gil a form to fill out which he did without specifying any kind of injury. He wrote only that he had been in an accident the previous day and that he had been sent there by the ambulance chaser.

A nurse took his vital signs. "Were you injured?"

"I don't know. My lawyer sent me."

"You don't know if you're injured?" She rolled her eyes. "Your lawyer probably suspects soft tissue injury. Sometimes you don't know you're injured until two or three days later. And then sometimes you suffer stress related to the accident. Doctor Wang will see you shortly."

Gil was left sitting on the examination table stripped to the waist. Dr. Wang entered the room and picked up the chart without even looking at Gil. "What kind of automobile accident did you have, Mr. Rodrigues?"

"Truck hit me while I was waiting for a light."

He felt Gil's neck, shoulders and spine. He had Gil lift his arms, swivel his head and touch his toes. "Any pain when you do this?'

"No, none."

"You have some limitation in your range of motion. Probably

soft tissue injury and whiplash. I will recommend a course of physical therapy." He scribbled a prescription, told Gil to get dressed, wrote something on the chart and left the room. It had all taken less than four minutes.

The prescription was for a prescription-level dosage of an over-the-counter painkiller.

His report wouldn't be enough to send Dr. Wang to jail, but it confirmed his client's suspicion of collusion between the ambulance chaser and the clinic. This lawyer and Dr. Wang would find it increasingly difficult to get money out of Gil's client company and if they pushed it too hard, and might find they had set themselves up for fraud charges.

There was no special urgency for Gil to hand in his report, but he needed money as always. As was his practice, he sent his bill with the report because the receivable was his major incentive to get the report written and mailed. He wrote and mailed this one within an hour of reaching his office.

Sabrina called. "Gotta tell you this before we get into my dad's phone bill. That Detective Chin called my mom. They arrested a 19-year-old—a Jesus Romero—with gang ties who's been doing carjackings with—he said—'the same MO'?" She made it a question.

"Guess you don't watch too many cop shows, honey. That's the way a criminal pulls off his crimes—his 'method of operating.' But it's encouraging to hear that."

"Well, I hope it's the right guy. I have to admit, Unc, I don't have a solid reason to suspect my dad's bosses. It was just my gut feel anyway, so who knows? Maybe some street character did it, after all. I appreciate what you've done so far."

"Let's not throw in the towel, yet. I've got a little momentum going here. It took a while and I'd hate to lose it. Let's dig a little further and watch developments with this Romero guy before we give it up. Ever get the phone bill?"

"I got the phone bill yesterday. Dad made six phone calls to the same LA area code number in the two days before his death."

"And you called the number?"

"I went a step further. My dad kept a business card holder. I looked for a match with the phone number. Ready for this? Consulate General's office, People's Republic of China in LA."

"Name on the card, Sabrina?"

"Let me just read it off for you: 'Shilin Quon, Commercial Consul, The People's Republic of China'. Each call was less than a minute. The last call was only about an hour before dad left for the temple. That call was nearly nine minutes long."

"When you dialed, who picked up—switchboard or Quon?"

"First time I got an answering machine with Quon's voice. The second time Quon picked up."

"Okay, the number rings at his desk. So when your dad called, either Quon wasn't available or—more likely—he ignored the first five calls, and he let his answering machine pick up. Then he takes call number six and your dad ends up dead in a few hours."

"So my dad left a message that got his attention?"

"Got Quon's attention and—I'm thinking—may have gotten your dad dead. I don't put much stock in coincidence. Sabrina, call Lieutenant Hara with this information. But wait a minute. Let me think." Gil paused. "Wait a couple of days before you call him. Just give him the phone bill and let him figure out who owns the number your dad was calling."

"Gotcha, Unc. Consul's at 501 Shatto Place in LA."

"Shatto? That's in the old Wilshire district as I recall. Later, honey. I want to talk with Tillman first."

Gil reached Tillman at his home. "The name Shilin Quon. Does that name ring a bell, Ron?"

"Couldn't have remembered it off the top of my head, but hearing it, it sounds like the guy from the Consulate—that diplomatic type I mentioned. I met him couple of times with Ming and his associate. I'm sure I have his card somewhere."

"And you said this consul type was pretty thick with our friends at DaleeAhn?"

"Yes, closed-door meetings—that kind of contact—with me sitting by myself as the outsider. Why do you ask?"

"Just an angle I'm working. Thanks, Ron. Can't talk now."

Gil phoned Steve Hara. "Sabrina tells me you have a suspect in her Dad's murder. That's great news."

"That's correct." Hara sounded pleased with himself. "Gang affiliation or background. Late teens. Hispanic. Gang and prison tattoos. But it gets even better."

"Better, Steve? Don't tell me you have a confession."

"That's exactly what we've got, old friend. It only took six hours, all videotaped, of course, but it's a confession."

"Good work. I hope it sticks."

"I'm sure it will. We've got a press conference scheduled for later today."

Gil phoned Sabrina. "I just talked to Hara. They got a confession out of Jesus—damned that sounds funny for some reason!" He chuckled at his irreverence. "They'll hold a press conference later."

"That's wonderful. I'll call Mom."

"Yes, but don't throw a party yet, honey. I'm just not sure on this one."

"How so, Unc?"

"I have to believe Hara knows what he's doing. But," Gil paused. "Don't you find it odd that this guy would be always jacking cars in mini-malls during the day? Then, he heads off to the parking lot of a Buddhist temple in the evening to jack a car in a custom color you could spot a mile away? Plus, just the presence of a guy in gang attire, haircut and tattoos there would attract attention all by itself."

"But he did confess, Unc."

"Yes, and he could have followed your dad to the temple, after cruising for Hondas with an accomplice in a spotter car. That's very possible, and, the more I think about it—probably the way it went down."

"So why your bad vibes about the confession?"

"From what I hear, they don't use a rubber hose any more, honey, but they do wear these kids down. And for the kids, jail time is just the cost of doing business, so they'll confess just to get back to their cell and get some sleep."

"So the book gets closed on my dad's murder—with the wrong guy?"

"Evidently it happens, honey. How often, who knows? The DA promises no conviction on murder one if the suspect confesses. It's an easy conviction for the DA, who gets a tick mark in his conviction column."

"That's awful, Uncle Gil."

"That's the world as it is, honey, and always has been. Plenty of people who are lazy but politically ambitious in those jobs."

"So you're quitting now?"

"Not yet. It's just that I want to keep an open mind on this confession—at least for the moment. I've heard too many stories about these gang types. That said, I've got to hope he's the right guy so we can put your dad's murder to rest."

"To think of dad as the victim of a random street crime is just awful. You think it might be just that—a street crime?"

"We don't know yet, but I'm the guy who's always preaching the simple solution, so I'm the one who should have more confidence in the confession. We'll see. I'll feel better if I just dig around a little more before I throw in the towel."

"What do you have in mind, Unc?"

Gil composed his thoughts for a moment. "I see Hara as a politically shrewd and intelligent man, but I can't help but feel disappointed that he's crowing over this confession."

"It's all a little too easy, you're saying?"

"I'm saying it's not my place to warn Hara, but

I don't think it was smart of him to hold a press conference as if he just solved the crime of the century. He'll look silly if this Romero backpedals on his confession. The papers have run a number of articles about how juries these days have been sensitized by claims of police coercion."

"But the carjackings have stopped, haven't they?"

"The local ones, yes, so if the confession sticks, then I've got to be the first to congratulate Hara."

"What about Quon?"

"I've got to believe Quon there at the Consulate just might have more than a superficial interest in DaleeAhn and its operations. The bigger question for me though, is why your dad was so intent on speaking with Quon on the evening of his murder? Is that just coincidence?"

"And you haven't told any of this to Hara yet, have you?"

"I'll tell him if I develop anything significant. In the meantime, I'm going to talk with Quon. I've just got to check out that phone call. I'll try to see him tomorrow and hope he's in. Talk to you later, honey."

CHAPTER ELEVEN

Gil wanted to meet Quon face to face. A telephone call wouldn't suffice for what Gil had in mind. And Gil, with his background, could believe to a near certainty that virtually every phone call to a Chinese government office in the U.S. was intercepted and searched for keywords by one American intelligence agency or another. Gil assumed that the Chinese swept their offices on a regular basis for bugs planted by American spooks. He preferred any meeting he was to have with Quon not be recorded, but if it were, he didn't care. He would take that chance because he wasn't doing anything illegal so far as he knew. Quon, on the other hand, would have to be cautious, especially if he had been party to a crime.

The neighborhood of the Consulate General of the People's Republic of China in Los Angeles lay only a few blocks east of Koreatown. The area, part of the Wilshire Boulevard corridor, had at one time been considered posh or exclusive. White flight to the suburbs in the 60's had changed all of that, giving the area, like so many of LA's neighborhoods, a bleak look. Pedestrian traffic was all but absent. Office buildings that had once housed law firms, medical offices and countless other businesses were either empty or only partially occupied. Businesses that had stayed in the area had done so only for cheap rents or political reasons. If it weren't for city, county, state and federal agencies that occupied a great deal of office space in this and other areas bordering downtown LA, even more buildings would be unoccupied.

And, to make the neighborhood even less attractive, that section of LA was home to the notorious Eighteenth Street Gang, said to be an arm of the Mexican Mafia, and its rival gang Mara Salvatrucha, whose origins were in the streets of El Salvador. Police controlled but could never put a complete stop to the turf warfare between the two rival gangs.

Except for the Chinese flag atop the building and the red and gold escutcheon of the PRC over the front door, the building was nearly indistinguishable from the others on that part of Shatto Place. The receptionist spoke English with only a slight accent. “Do you have an appointment with Mr. Quon? I believe he’s in, but I’m not sure if he’s available.”

“Give him my card. Tell him I need to talk to him about David Chang. He will be available.” Gil gave a slight stress to the word “will.”

Gil was kept waiting, during which time he browsed Chinese pamphlets printed in English and stacked in racks hung in the reception area. After about ten minutes, a young woman emerged from the office area and ushered Gil into a small conference room, where he took a seat at the conference table facing the door. She offered him tea or coffee, which he politely declined.

After less than three minutes, Shilin Quon, Commercial Consul, entered the room. Gil stood to accept his handshake, and then they sat opposite. Quon was dressed, as one would expect a diplomat to be dressed, in a well-fitted pinstriped navy blue suit and vest, matching tie, and what Gil guessed were jade cuff links. Quon was taller than the average Chinese man by about four inches. His hair was jet black and close cropped. His handsome face put him in the company of film actors who played aristocrats in costume dramas on Asian cable TV.

“Mr. Rodrigues, how nice to meet you. I postponed the start of my next meeting. I regret I can only give you few minutes.” Quon’s smile was expansive and seemed to come naturally. His

English carried only the slightest accent. He clearly had the charm and worldliness for the job. As far as what other talents, training or political connections qualified him for a position as consul, Gil could only speculate.

"Thanks for seeing me, Mr. Quon. If time is short, then I'll get straight to why I'm here."

"You mentioned David Chang? It's just awful. I'm so sorry I could not attend the funeral. I was acquainted with him, you know. It is reassuring to know that the authorities have found his murderer."

"With all my heart I hope they have, but I still have questions of my own. You spoke with him on the phone the evening he was killed."

"I speak with so many people. I can't be sure."

Gil looked directly into Quon's eyes. "Let's you and I not say silly things to each other. I have a record of the calls. For personal reasons I want to know what you talked about with my friend David. The police will ask you for professional reasons."

"An assistant may have answered the call. I'm not sure I recall . . . "

Gil cut him off. "Mr. Quon, you realize, of course, that U.S. Customs people may want to look at some of that equipment Ming and his friends have been exporting—most likely to China—through that friendly freight forwarder."

"Freight? I don't know what you're talking about Mr. Rodrigues."

"You're a very intelligent man, Mr. Quon. Were you a classmate of Ming's at the Beijing College of International Relations? Only the brightest and the most well connected go there—isn't that right? Then it's off to steal what you can of other people's technology to use or copy."

Quon seemed to have caught his breath before saying, "You've certainly done your homework, Mr. Rodrigues."

"That and then some, but your college credentials were—quite frankly—an assumption on my part."

"And, like any good investigator, you've tested that assumption, haven't you?"

Without raising his hand off the table, Gil pointed a finger at Quon. "Look, I don't give a damn about your high-tech shopping spree, even though I can't get it out of my head that David's death might be related to it in some way. I want to know why David called you the night he was killed."

Quon pushed away a few inches from the conference table, took a deep breath, laid his palms down on the table and looked at the wall. He said nothing for a half minute and then turned to look at Gil. "It's part of my job to facilitate trade with my country. A lot of Chinese—yes, and American businessmen, too—want my attention. I can't deal with all of them."

"But my witnesses say you spent a lot of time with Ming and his venture."

"My government—or, rather, one of The People's corporations—has a significant monetary investment in DaleeAhn. I would be irresponsible if I didn't make myself available for whatever help I could give them."

"Mr. Quon, you're still dancing around an answer to my question."

"Yes, maybe I am. David seemed to like me. He always wanted to—how do you say, 'bend my ear'—when I visited his office or attended a company dinner. He was always offering some suggestion or other about how DaleeAhn should handle its finances, but I would politely suggest he offer his ideas to his CEO, Mr. Ming."

"Did he ever suggest anything was amiss at DaleeAhn?"

"Amiss? I'm not sure, but he seemed to think that I had a lot more authority or—how do you say—'clout' than I, in fact, do. Frankly, I think he was impressed by my title."

"What did he complain about?"

"Nothing specific. He would hint at things that were 'inappropriate' at times, but I chose not to get involved in the internal affairs of what is, legally, a California corporation even though it has formed a joint venture with a Chinese company."

"And the night he was killed? He called you about something 'inappropriate'?"

"He said it was vitally important he meet with me. He said it was too important to talk about on the phone. I think he even mentioned his daughter at one point. He was very excited. I suggested he come here, but he said he felt safer if we met at some place like the Buddhist Temple near his home."

"And you agreed to meet him at the temple?"

"Yes, but I didn't go even though I had fully intended to when I had agreed to it. After I hung up with him, I felt he was being melodramatic about who knows what and decided not to meet him after all."

"And you called Ming?"

"NO!" Quon slapped the table. "I did NOT call Ming!" Quon's chest heaved as he caught his breath and recovered his composure.

"You didn't have to because he called you?"

Quon paused before speaking in measured tones. "Mr. Ming called me on a regular basis—two, three times a week, always around the time that David had just happened to call early that evening. Callers know that's a good time to catch you at your desk." Again he paused and looked at Gil. "He called me about thirty minutes after David called me. He wanted me to meet him for dinner at some place with 'bar hostesses.' I wasn't up to it. It's not my kind of entertainment."

"And you asked him to see David in your place?"

"Yes."

"And he said he would?"

"No, only that he would try and that he didn't know if he would have the time. He didn't commit to seeing him. He seemed unconcerned. Said something about David's 'hysteria.' That's my word. He used the Mandarin word meaning nervous excitement."

"How did you learn of David's death?"

"Ming called me the next day. He said that when David hadn't reported to work, he called his home and learned of David's death from his wife."

"And that was a vanilla conversation because you both know your phone calls are likely being monitored around the clock."

"How do you know these things, Mr. Rodrigues?"

"I read a lot."

"Mr. Rodrigues, let me offer this for what it's worth: Mr. Ming and I—as you say—'go back a way' and you've already guessed at that. Both of our fathers were good friends. Both were powerful men in China and both died in a way and for reasons I do not wish to discuss."

"You're going to tell me that Ming was not capable of murdering David?"

"Close. You and I know almost anything's possible in this world, but I can't imagine my friend driving to a Buddhist temple and murdering someone."

"Which doesn't rule out his hiring someone."

Quon looked at the table. "As I said, anything's possible, but I don't believe he'd do that. I truly don't. And now I have to get to my meeting. I have people waiting."

After the meeting with Quon, Gil drove to the LA Public Library. If he found what he thought he might find somewhere in the library, he wasn't sure what he would do with it anyway, but he would worry about that later. Gil was still running on instinct, because he had, after all, no formal training as a homicide investigator. An idiot could solve a crime with fingerprints, blood, semen, fibers, confessions or eyewitnesses he told himself, but in this case he felt at no intellectual disadvantage. Right or wrong, Gil was confident that Lieutenant Hara would continue to treat this case like a common street crime and sit content with the Romero confession, barring strong evidence to the contrary. If Hara did have the wrong guy, it would become a cold case. But to Gil, unlike Hara, this was personal.

Gil rarely met a reference desk librarian he didn't like, but then maybe it was all in the approach. He had learned that in grad school. If the person had been trained as a librarian and wasn't just some kid working part time, then he or she seemed to like the job. He avoided a younger woman and approached the svelte and forty-something looking female at the reference counter. She wore no wedding ring and was still in the loving years. Her one-piece dress was tasteful and snug, but not painted on. Her nails were manicured, her dark brown hair bobbed in the manner of many women her age. The word "divorced" could have been stenciled on her forehead and Gil conceived a mini-fantasy of spending an evening with her slow dancing to build in her sense of anticipation. The stage directions in that fantasy called for her to have a whale of a good time when he took her home. He wondered idly if she had a lover.

He was counting on the proximity in their ages and he laid it on thick—not too thick he hoped. He flashed his PI license at her, half covering it with his hand. He watched her dark pupils dilate. It was just like in the movies, she would tell her friends. He leaned on the counter, spoke in conspiratorial tones and told her how he knew she would understand the need for confidentiality and all that. On the other hand, if he were at liberty to tell her, then he was sure she would recognize the name of the prominent person who had retained his services.

He had whispered the word "prominent" and maintained the conspiratorial tone. "News clippings from mainland China going back, say, ten, fifteen years—what can you do for me?" She pursed her lips at the question.

Whether she bought into Gil's scam or was just showing that she, too, could flirt was impossible to tell, but she gave him one of those knowing nods and a half-wink that only forty-something women could deliver so well. She emulated the same tone of conspiracy. "Be right back." She made three trips for three volumes. "Here's a start."

The books had titles such as *Survey of People's Republic of China Press* and *Weekly Digest of Asian Events* and *U.S. Foreign Broadcast Information Service: Daily Report.*

Gil thanked the woman. "My name's Gil. What's yours?"

She smiled. "It's Raquel."

"Raquel, can you be bribed?"

"Excuse me?"

"It's lunch on me if you help me find something. What I'm looking for may not go back that far. I'm guessing within the last five or six years."

Gil's powers of persuasion worked. The librarian agreed to search one volume while Gil searched another. He asked her to look for captions or headlines dealing with indictments or prosecution in China for corruption or embezzlement involving one or both of two men—named Quon and Ming.

At the moment Gil saw was no urgency to the search, for it was based merely on a hunch. Yet Gil wanted to test that hunch so as to get back to earning a living if his search didn't yield anything. After about twenty-five minutes, Raquel appeared to regret having agreed to help, but she persisted anyway. Whether it was just luck or greater experience she found it.

"Two Former Intelligence Chiefs Convicted," read the headline. The story continued, "Liko Quon and Deshi Ming, both former officers in Chinese Intelligence were convicted of corruption, bribe-taking and embezzlement of public funds. Both men, according to prosecutors, had taken bribes from smugglers earlier convicted for bringing luxury cars into China for years without paying duties. The two men were also convicted of taking kickbacks from Chinese businessmen and foreigners hoping to be given favorable treatment in business ventures. The Discipline Inspection Committee of the Central Committee of the Communist Party had prosecuted the case after army anti-corruption investigators tried to bury the matter. Quon and Ming were sentenced to death."

When Gil asked Raquel for change to use the copy machine, she simply used her own machine to copy the page for Gil.

Gil thanked her for her valuable assistance and left. She had declined lunch, but offered a vague "maybe another time." On the ride back he felt pleased with himself. It felt good to follow a hunch and find you were right. He would assume Quon had some oversight responsibility with regard to the use of funds at DaleeAhn. And, it was clear that Quon and Ming had a firm bond founded on common experience: They had been classmates in an elite school. Moreover, both of their fathers had made untimely departures from planet earth on the wrong end of a bullet. Whether that bond between the two men led to murder remained to be seen. Of one thing, however, Gil was certain: The risks their fathers had taken to pocket some of The People's money weren't risks to be taken by the faint-hearted.

CHAPTER TWELVE

Gil phoned Sabrina Chang at work. "You and your mom home tonight? We need to look through your dad's home office."

"Yes, how about seven or so? By the way, Mom and I are grateful for what you're doing, Uncle Gil."

"Don't be too effusive in your thanks, honey. It's been only a part-time effort and I've nothing to show for it yet. I've got clients to serve and a living to make. It's not like in the movies where the PI drops everything to catch the killer, much as I'd like to do that."

"Do what you have to, Unc; we're still grateful. See you tonight."

Today Gil would do his second assignment, the job-stress claims. The job that day would earn him a nice fee, but required some ham acting on his part. To prepare himself, Gil had been letting his beard grow for two days. Before leaving home, he put on a pair of paint-splattered jeans, scruffy tennis shoes, a worn shirt and a Bruins baseball cap that was badly in need of a wash. Around his neck he hung a voice-activated mini-cassette recorder.

That day Gil was after a "capper" and the doctors and lawyers for whom the capper worked. Most people have never heard of a capper even if they are aware of what he does for a living. A capper is paid, under the table, for finding and sending clients to unscrupulous lawyers. Some cappers might have police scanners that would enable them to drive to the scene of an accident to hand out a lawyer's business card. Frequently, insurance companies would find that all the passengers on a bus involved in a minor accident just happened to be represented by the same lawyer, whose offices were remarkably distant from the plaintiffs' neighborhoods. And often there would be more plaintiffs than there were passengers on the bus at the time of the accident.

Other cappers would stand in front of unemployment offices, to find and encourage people who had lost jobs to file false workers' compensation claims for illnesses manufactured by lawyers and doctors. One of the latter was the subject of Gil's assignment that day. His activities provided Gil with an opportunity to collect another check from the insurance company that was trying to assess and control fraudulent claims.

Gil's client knew only that this capper called himself "Luis" and hung out in front of the state unemployment office in Whittier. Gil circled the block three times before parking. The unemployment office was a place that people who had just been laid off visited, filed their claims, and left. They didn't hang around the sidewalk in front, so he had to hope that the man who was hanging out there was "Luis," talking to his target.

Gil entered the building without making eye contact with the man. He spent fifteen minutes in a waiting area pretending to read and another five in front of a bulletin board with job postings. People filing real claims left with paperwork so Gil grabbed some forms from the counter, then rolled them up to obscure their contents and went outside. Back on the sidewalk, he again avoided eye contact with the man he hoped was Luis.

The man wore dark sunglasses and a blue plaid shirt that hung over his belt. His hair was cropped closer than a Marine's. The legs of his pants nearly touched the ground. He looked vaguely Chicano. "Looking for something?"

Gil looked at the man. "Oh. Yeah. Never been to this office. Looking for some place I can get some coffee. Got a cigarette? Need to pick up a pack."

"Coffee shop block up on your right." The man pulled a half-pack of Marlboros from his pants pocket, shook two free from the pack and offered a light to Gil before lighting his own. "First time out of work?"

The man was now standing next to Gil. "No, but first time in a while." Gil affected nervousness with the cigarette. He hoped he had set the sensitivity level just right on the cassette recorder under his shirt.

The man drew on the cigarette, and then crushed it on the sidewalk after the one puff. "If you don't mind my saying, my friend, you look a little stressed."

"Hard to say." Gil deliberately puffed his cigarette like a person not used to smoking. "No fun to get laid off. Got bills to pay like everybody else."

"If you want to make some side money, I can send you to a lawyer I know who can help you find a doctor for your stress."

"Stress? You mean like nerves? How's that make me money?"

"Ever heard of workers' comp or job stress? My lawyer friend gets money for people all the time."

"This is all new to me." Gil's cigarette was already half smoked and he crushed it out. "So I see this lawyer and what?"

"He tells you what to say to the doctor. You can't sleep; you're nervous and depressed. Know what I'm sayin'? The doctor writes a report and the lawyer files a comp claim for you."

"Just like that?"

The man pulled a business card from his shirt pocket and scribbled on it. "Tell you what, if you show up today, fifty dollars, no questions asked. Comes out of the money the lawyer gets for you. Sound interesting?"

Gil took the card from the man and looked at it. It was an address in Whittier. "What did you say the doctor's name was?"

"I didn't say."

"Just wondered if he's not too far from my home."

"Name's Dr. Hamoodi. His office is next door to my lawyer friend. That makes it easy."

"Thanks. Your name?"

"Luis." Luis slapped Gil on the back and offered his hand. Gil smiled at the man as he shook his hand.

Gil drove the short distance to the lawyer's office, parked, and entered the building next door to get the full name, address and suite number of Dr. Hamoodi from the tenant directory. His report would be short, but he would bill his client for another five hours. Gil would see the lawyer Luis suggested and Dr. Hamoodi on another day. He was becoming preoccupied with David's murder.

It was only slightly past noon. He made a quick change with the extra clothing he always kept at the office. He was off to county offices in Norwalk. Gil had some homework to do before looking at David's records. He would write his report to the insurance company tomorrow. Instead of going back to his office, he drove to the Los Angeles County recorder's office in Norwalk. There he took the elevator to the Business Filings and Registration unit. He looked for fictitious business names that had been registered as sole proprietorships or partnerships by anyone named Ming, Quon or Liao at about the time that DaleeAhn had been incorporated. In less than thirty minutes he found three: Dali Star Enterprises, South Coast Ventures and Teal Promotions had all been filed and recorded on the same date within days of DaleeAhn's incorporation. All three were sole proprietorships with the owner listed as Zhiyuan Ming. The Proofs of Publication indicated that the public notices were published in an obscure suburban weekly in one of the beach cities. Gil had seen this done before; it was a common ploy of embezzlers. The fictitious, doing-business-as name registrations would have allowed Ming to open a separate bank account in the name of each of the business names. From there on out, everything was relatively simple—at least in execution. Ming needed only to create, and then approve, the payment of phony invoices to siphon company funds into bank accounts he owned. His nearest oversight or potential audit was probably in China.

Gil paid the clerk a small fee for certified copies of the three fictitious business registrations. He then drove to the street address that the three shared. He had noted that while the suite numbers were different, the "daytime phone number" was the same for all three.

It was as Gil suspected. The address was a storefront business in a mini-mall that provided private mailboxes, parcel post and shipping services. The signs in the window offered 500 business cards with stationery for forty-nine-ninety-five and international money orders for Mexico, South America, Taiwan and India.

The suite numbers for each of the three businesses were nothing more than numbers to individual mailboxes. From a pay phone, Gil called the phone number for the businesses. It was as he had anticipated. The type of ring indicated it was a voice mail service rather than an answering machine, and the voice on the greeting was clearly that of Jeff Ming. Gil said nothing and hung up.

Now, if the DaleeAhn accounting records David had kept at home showed payments to these entities that existed only on paper, it made Ming an embezzler. Whether it made him a murderer, too, remained to be seen.

It was now nearly 4:30 P.M. By the time Gil got back to his neighborhood, it would be time for a drink. He turned for the Sunset Room, a fixture in town for thirty years. That made it primordial by California standards. It was time to sit among some familiar faces, even if they were mostly acquaintances and not friends. It was time for his two drinks and some sports and bar talk. The once-upscale neighborhood had deteriorated around the bar, which sat between a Tae Kwon Do school and a video game store. The customers, waitresses and bartenders computed their patronage and tenure in decades.

The bartenders used no gadgets to measure a precise ounce or jigger for each drink. They preferred to just eyeball it and the owner liked it that way; it kept his customers coming back to kill their pain. The food didn't qualify as haute cuisine, but its meats and fish were fresh, tasty, and reasonably priced. Gil and his late wife had made eating there a weekly ritual Fridays after work.

Gil found a stool next to a man he knew only as Tom.

Tom seemed to be there whenever the bar was open, six days per week. Gil was certain that if the Bureau of Labor ever made "Bar Patron" a legitimate occupational title, then surely Tom could claim it.

Tom was lying in wait to ambush someone to chat with. Gil walked into it, as he had done before, but didn't mind. Tom often made for informed conversation.

"I see they nailed someone in the Chang murder," Tom said.

"Yes, I read it the *Tribune*."

"Are you trying to find the killer yourself? You and David were good friends as I recall."

"Yes, good friends. And, no, I wouldn't get involved in a police matter." It was easier to lie.

"Gil, can I ask you a personal question?"

"Knowing you, Tom, you'll ask anyway."

"I always wanted to know how in hell did you ever become a PI? Seems so out of character for you."

"And what kind of character is that—a bad character maybe?"

"Seriously, Gil. You don't seem to have a cop's mentality. You seem kind of—I don't know—brainy—for the job." Tom's tone made it a question.

"I'm being a wise ass, but I think I know what you mean. It's a good question. I don't know if I have a good answer."

"You stumbled into it?"

"Stumbled, fell, ran—that's as good as I can come up with."

"You needed a job like the rest of us?"

"Needed a job when I got out of the Army. Took what I thought would be a temporary job doing fraud work for an insurance company. You know the routine—'until I found something better'."

"And you found the something better?"

"Six years and two kids later I left for greener pastures in the world of marketing capital goods."

"I see where you're headed, Gil. Those greener pastures turned brown, as they did for a lot of us."

"No epiphany. No sunbeam breaking through the clouds or stained glass windows. If I entered a church the walls would develop cracks."

Tom grinned. "You mean no big revelation with a choir singing?"

"Oh, there's a moment I suppose."

"And yours?"

"My boss was a psychopath in a three-piece suit. He treated the men like dogs and the women like chambermaids, but he gave me a wide berth. Why, I don't know."

Tom let out a "Hah!" and slapped the padded elbow rest.

Gil stared at him as if he were looking at a square egg. "What's so funny?"

Tom shook his head. "Because he knew you'd throw him under a bus—that's why." He laughed at his own remark.

Gil ignored the remark and continued. "There's always that moment. He told me to fire a guy that I knew didn't deserve firing. He just didn't like the guy. I managed to get the guy transferred to another division. He was too old to find comparable work somewhere else."

"And that wasn't enough for your boss?"

"No, he wanted me to destroy the man."

"So he fired you instead?"

"He tried to. He trumped up a poor performance report on me, but I told him to stuff it where the sun doesn't shine and refused to sign it. I took it over his head to his boss. He was told to back off, but I had made a mortal enemy."

"At some level they know those guys are wackos, but I guess they make money for the company," Tom said.

"Nothing wrong with making money. But that about tore it. By that time, I had already worked for one other crazy, so I knew there would be others after him this year or next until I got 're-structured' out of a job—or I punched one of these creeps in the nose for terrorizing some secretary."

"So you upped and quit?" Tom asked.

"Not right away. I needed the job. I learned I had enough experience for a PI license, took the exam and hung out a shingle a few months later."

"And the business just rolled in?"

"Enough rolled in after I undercut the big firms."

"I get it—the low overhead routine. 'Keeps our prices low'."

"Hell, I had no shame by then. Low overhead is good."

"And it's worked out?"

"It's better than a poke in the eye with a sharp stick. Don't know if I ever will—or care—to sort it out, but I think it all has to do with what we expect out of life."

"Expect from life? You're getting heavy, Gil, and this is only our second drink."

"There were days I thought Helen would kill me because I left the corporate world, but bless her heart she went along with it even though we weren't getting rich."

"Yeah, wives can be so damned practical. Spoils all the fun."

"I think she went along with it because we both grew up poor. A professor of mine liked to say that minimal aspirations are the curse of growing up poor."

"Your professor got it right, Gil. Hey, since we're both feeling so damned philosophical, let's not you and I forget that work is the curse of the drinking class." Tom signaled the bartender for two more.

"Two's my limit today, friend, drinking class or no."

"Since it's my turn to pay, here's another one I always meant to ask."

"You're a royal pain in the ass, you know. So what's this other damned question?"

"You use an ankle holster?"

Gil rolled his eyes. "You're another one who's seen too many movies."

"What? Ya ain't packin' heat?" Tom was proud of his gangster accent.

"I don't even own a gun."

"You're kidding me. I thought … "

"You thought wrong, old buddy. In California PI's have to have a permit to carry a concealed weapon. Plus, I never did any work that needed a gun."

"You've shattered the image, Gil."

"Sorry about that. If it makes you feel any better, I know how to load them and which end to point at the bad guys. Does that count?"

"Oh, before I forget," Tom said. "Whatever happened to your boss?"

"He kept getting promoted. Eventually he left and became CEO of a Fortune 500 company. He's crazy mean, but he makes money for the stockholders and could charm the pants off any woman alive. They even interview him on CNN from time to time. He re-invents himself every couple of years and holds 'leadership conferences' where he dispenses his wisdom."

"Amazing," Tom said. "And by now he believes his own press releases, I'd guess."

"He does indeed, Tom. Gotta go, old buddy."

After Gil left Tom he picked up a copy of the *Tribune* and saw some familiar faces on the front page. "Town Leaders Laud Sheriff in Temple Murder Case," read the headline. The photo showed four persons posing for the camera, a woman and two men sitting with Lieutenant Hara. One of the men owned a small food market; the other was a podiatrist. All three had recently made clear their plans to run for the school board.

So far as Gil knew, none had been even acquainted with David; nevertheless, there they were milking some publicity out of his murder and the arrest of Jesus Romero for the crime. "No one in the community had been safe," the trio insisted in the context of the story, "until David's killer was caught."

Sandy Jackson, housewife, school cafeteria aide and candidate for school board, encouraged everyone in the community to take extra precautions when approaching one's car and to report any suspicious persons. Sam Yee and Ronald Houk, the two men, said they hoped that David's murder was not racially motivated because that would give the community a bad name. Steve Hara said he wanted to assure the three community leaders that his team would continue to take all steps necessary to protect the community from this and similar crimes.

Gil knew that Hara was competent enough to handle this kind of nonsense. Of all people, Hara would know that its real intent was a self-serving and vulgar self-promotion, but Gil couldn't help feel a pang of sympathy for him and couldn't wait to tell him so. He would, however, have to wait a day or two to do so.

In the meantime, Gil was eager to know what he and Sabrina might find in David's home office.

CHAPTER THIRTEEN

From the moment he had heard the news, Gil asked himself over and over: what had brought David to be put to death, like a criminal, at that particular time and place near the Buddhist temple, where he had spent so much time looking for Truth? Gil wasn't looking for The Truth or the Great White Whale. He just wanted to find David's killer, but for all he knew at this point, that killer was sitting, fully confessed, in the county jail. And, Gil's disregard of that reality was beginning to make him wonder if he wasn't becoming obsessive—or just plain irrational—in looking to answer a question that had already been answered. After further thought, however, he justified his persistence by telling himself that he didn't have all that much time invested anyway and, if he quit now, he would never believe he had done all that he could have for David's widow, sister and daughter.

It struck Gil that David must have lived his life a fatalist. He wondered if being a Buddhist made one a fatalist. He didn't know and at the moment didn't care; he would look it up some time. Whatever its source, David's worldview suggested that he thought everything that happened was scripted in a big book somewhere. David would have written off his own death to fate, and regarded his killer as merely the instrument of that fate.

Gil didn't believe in fate except as metaphor after the fact, but he did believe in an irrational world and in free will. If he had taken the trouble to verbalize it, Gil might have said that people were all products of their pasts and if they look, they would find connections between choices they made and events in their pasts and how their lives turned out—or ended.

Gil's conversation with Quon was driving him, and he thought that he would do some snooping that evening among David's records and in his computer. After that, he would see what he could learn about David's past.

Outwardly, David Chang's house was little different from hundreds of others in the community, one of the few suburbs in Los Angeles County not yet incorporated into a city. The layout of the house was cookie-cutter, a four-bedroom ranch style on a street less than two miles from the Buddhist temple David had visited weekly. He had converted one bedroom into an office, one into a den. Sabrina had her own apartment, but had been staying with her mother Mei in the house since the funeral in a temporary arrangement.

Gil hadn't been in David's house in many months. He had nearly forgotten how much he admired the simple, uncluttered good taste of the furnishings so common in Asian homes. For David and his wife, those furnishings included black or light tan leather upholstery, black or white enameled side tables and cabinetry with genuine brass hardware, stark lamps, Asian landscapes on the walls, and tasteful bric-a-brac of mostly Chinese origin. The floors were polished wood tile with an occasional area rug. Both the living room and David's office had statues of the Buddha. The house was spotless. One left one's shoes in the foyer.

One wall of the den housed an eclectic collection of books and CD's. Earlier visits to the Chang home and conversations with David told Gil that David actually read the books in his collection. He seemed to favor books dealing with spiritual and mystical subjects, but he read his history, literature, and science, too. And David was proud of having made a significant dent in his Great Books collection.

David and Mei once confided to Gil that they had chosen their house and organized the furnishings according to the principles of "feng shui." They tried hard to explain it to Gil, but with questionable success. As best as Gil could understand, it was the Chinese practice of organizing one's surroundings to increase the flow of "chi" or energy.

They offered to do the same for the flow of chi in Gil's house and office. He told them he needed as much chi as they could generate for him, but politely deferred their offer to some indefinite future time. He told them that, in the meantime, he would have to hope that the chi was flowing unhindered through his surroundings.

Mei Chang served tea and almond cookies in the living room. She had been nearly silent since Gil arrived. "We haven't taken anything from David's office since he died."

Mei had a hint of moisture in her eyes that were reddened by tears. She had been a housewife for all of her married years so her English wasn't polished as David's had been. Nevertheless, she spoke clearly and with dignity.

"David—Danjun—his Chinese name—took this job as an accountant for DaleeAhn when they started eight months ago. He was very happy. Then, about two months ago, he started to worry, to be nervous." She paused.

Sabrina said, "I've heard this—sorry to say not until my dad died, but you need to hear it, too."

"And you asked him what was wrong, Mei?" Gil asked.

"Yes. He said only that he was very busy, but I knew something was wrong—maybe something bad. He hated his boss and job. He went to his office here in house at night. He worked with his computer. He always looked worried."

"And the night he died, Mei?"

"He said he was meeting someone at the temple, but did not say who."

"But he usually went there every Thursday night for his study class?" Gil asked.

"Yes," she said, "but that same night—Thursday—he said he was meeting someone."

"And when he didn't come home you called the sheriff."

Mei looked down. "Yes."

The three sat silent for several moments. Gil sipped his tea, but left most of it in the cup. He changed the subject. "You're saying it's okay for me to go through David's records? I'm hoping something in those records will point us someplace."

"I'll help best I can, Uncle Gil. It was my idea to do this. And Mom, I don't want you hovering over us, please." All three remained subdued through tea.

David's home office reflected his personality, a personality that included a dimension of compulsion, a trait most certainly useful in accounting. Everything was in its place. The desk was made of black enameled wood and was built to house a computer with a keyboard tray and CPU compartment. A monitor sat on the desk surface. To the right was a calculator with a roll tape. The metal file cabinets were also black.

"You read my mind," Gil said to Sabrina when she handed him a martini. He took a sip and made an exaggerated pucker. "Oooh! Delish! Thanks, honey. Where'd you learn how to mix such a good martini?"

She smiled. "Women's dorm."

"Didn't know your dad kept booze around."

"He didn't. I picked up the mixings and some beer on the way over. I'm going have a beer myself." She bent down and turned on the computer, then took a pull on her beer while the machine cranked up. She invited Gil to take David's chair while she grabbed a folding chair, placed it to Gil's right and then sat down next to him.

"The 'Search' function is about the sum total of my computer knowledge, Sabrina. Good place to start?" Neither spoke as Gil typed "account" into the window and clicked "Find Now." It brought up a long list of files.

After some minutes, they found folders with some accounting shorthand. These broke down further into files with labels such as "AP," "GL," and "AR." Sabrina used a pencil to guide their eyes over items on the screen as they scrolled through files and folders with labels like "cash," "assets," "expenses," and the other accounting terms. While neither of them had been trained as an accountant, both understood the basic accounting model and its terminology.

One item caught their attention. It was the initial capitalization from what appeared to be a parent company and a draw on the Bank of China for five million dollars via wire transfer.

"Sabrina, I did some checking today on a hunch. I stopped by the LA County recorder's office. I'll tell you about it if my hunch turns out to be on target. Let's look at the accounts payable and expenses before we look anywhere else. And I want to look at hard copy here in your dad's file drawers.

They found the hard copy after several minutes and scanned it. There were the usual payments for utilities, supplies, and car leasing companies, and some large payments to machine tool distributors. They scrolled through the payments. None of Ming's phony business names appeared among those payments for nearly the first eight weeks of DaleeAhn's existence. Toward the end of the second month, however, Ming's fictitious company names began to appear in the payables. The first one to appear was to Teal Promotions for nine thousand dollars and some change for "promotional development."

"Bingo, Sabrina!"

"You see something I don't, Unc?"

"Does the name or word 'teal' have any significance in Chinese culture? I always thought it was some kind of duck. Why do I think I've heard that somewhere?"

"I've heard of it, but I've never seen the stuff. My dad told me once that 'teal' is a type of gold coinage. It's like an Asian private currency. He said the older Asian immigrant types who don't trust banks use it. Or maybe they want to hide profits from the tax man." They looked toward Mei Chang who was listening and nodding her head in agreement.

"So Ming has a sense of humor, too, even about his own little swindles."

"How so, Unc?"

"I told you I had done some homework today at the Recorder's Office. Ming has three phony business names registered. One of them he calls Teal Promotions. The other two are Dali Star Enterprises and South Coast Ventures."

"So you expect to find more payments to himself if we keep scrolling?"

Gil couldn't hide his excitement and he watched Sabrina's eyes widen. "Let's keep on scrollin', scrollin', scrollin'." It was to the tune of "Rawhide." They both laughed at the lame humor.

In the first several months alone, they found several hundreds of thousands of dollars that had been paid to Ming's fictitious companies. The payment details always listed some sort of soft service such as "promotional work," "consulting" or "product research." They also found account numbers for gold and platinum credit cards coupled with payments for expenses and large cash advances incurred on those cards.

Gil looked at the credit card balances and whistled. "These guys lived high off the hog."

"Look at the entries for casinos, restaurants and hotels," Sabrina said. "And what are these huge expenditures for machine tools, manufacturing and design software? Wow!"

"We can be sure he came here with a shopping list," Gil said.

Sabrina began riffling through David's file drawers. After several minutes she pulled out a manila folder. "This could be interesting, Unc. It's labeled 'Bank Accounts'."

Gil and Sabrina were almost gleeful as they fumbled through the files.

"Look at this, honey." Gil fanned the sheets out on the desk. They were photocopies of bank statements. "Wow! Three bank accounts, one for each of Ming's fictitious businesses, with nothing but deposits. I'll bet these deposits match the payments made from the accounts payable."

"So what do you make of it all?"

"I'm certainly not a forensic accountant, but it looks like Ming stuck to his shopping list, but did some textbook embezzlement along the way," Gil said.

"Is it a motive for murder?"

"If he thought your dad might blow the whistle on him, it could be plenty of motive."

"But my dad would have to be part of any kind of embezzlement, wouldn't he?"

"That could get tricky. Paying some invoices approved by his boss could be innocent enough, I suppose. Question is whether your dad helped cook the books for the parent company in China."

"Do you think my dad would do that?"

"He wouldn't do it voluntarily. There was no gain in it for him other than just to go along to get along and keep his job and his paycheck. And we certainly don't know of any second accountant."

Sabrina looked toward her mother, who looked at the floor.

"Sabrina—before I forget—would you be kind enough to make some copies of these records in the next few days? Somehow, I think I'll have use for them in one way or another."

Gil was elated about his discoveries in David's office and on his computer. The next morning Gil couldn't resist the impulse to needle Hara about the *Tribune* story and his press conference. He phoned Hara who greeted Gil's call with feigned annoyance. "Don't tell me you're running for school board, too."

Gil laughed. "No, Steve, just calling to express my sympathy for the crap you have to put up with in your job. I saw the story in the *Trib.*"

Gil could hear Hara groan before he said; "I can use all the sympathy you've got after a session with that ditzoid housewife, grocery clerk, and foot doctor. You know, I can admire the smart and ambitious, but when they're dumb and ambitious, it makes me want to puke."

Gil laughed. "I've been developing some theories on my own, Steve."

Hara jumped in. "I warned you, if you learn anything … "

Gil cut him off. "Steve, give it a rest. If I learn anything solid, I'll tell you. You know that."

"By now I hope you do."

"Steve … " Gil paused. "We know Romero is a carjacker. His victims all identified him. Could he also be a killer hired to make a killing look like a botched carjacking?"

"Again, Gil, to get back to our conversation of the other day, if you're of the 'anything's possible' school, then I guess it's possible. So why do you ask? Do you know something I don't?"

"No, I was just speculating."

Gil knew he was bending the truth with that statement, but it would do for now while he continued his own pursuit of David's killer or killers. He would tell Hara about David's books in due time.

Right now it was time to talk with David's sister Diana. It was time to explore David's past.

CHAPTER FOURTEEN

Gil had found David's copies of DaleeAhn's books far more interesting than he would have imagined, even though his discovery of Ming's fictitious business names had led him to expect he would find embezzlement.

Now it was time to explore any links between David's past and the present. Again, Gil had to remind himself that the killer was probably sitting in jail. Another one of his hunches, however, dictated that a connection with China might have played a part in David's death. Gil had, however, little with which to test that hunch. He had only one major link to David's past and that link was David's sister, Diana.

David Chang had spent his childhood years on the other side of the globe in China. His parents were gone. Only Diana had known him since childhood in China, and Gil was counting on the fact that a man's sister might know things about him that a wife never will.

Diana Chang had been devastated by her brother's murder, but she met it with the stoicism one sees in cultures with a long history of famine and suffering. Gil would speak with her about David, but her stoic reserve might not be the only barrier to communication.

By now Gil's kids, David, David's widow and daughter knew that he and Diana had become more than mere friends and dinner companions. It was, after all, obvious in the way that the two looked at each other, disappeared some weekends, and communicated silently as only lovers can. Friends and family could see that both were still in the loving years and they seemed to be a good match in intellects and interests, despite an age gap that neither seemed to mind.

David had arranged a date between Gil and Diana about a year and a half after Gil's wife passed away. He pretended that his suggestion of a date had been just a casual thought and that he would first have to ask his sister if she was interested, but Gil knew David would have done that before even broaching the subject. Gil thought Diana might see him as too old for her, but David assured him that should not be a matter of concern to a woman of his culture. So David had set his trap into which Gil walked willingly, if not eagerly.

Her birth name was Wei Lin Chang, but her parents adopted the name of Diana for her, and David for her brother, when they came to the States because they were told that Diana and David were "strong" names. Years earlier, Diana Chang had become acquainted with Gil and his late wife through social gatherings involving the two families. She was taller than most Asians and while she didn't qualify as a great beauty in the Hollywood sense, she had learned to make the most of her physical qualities. Her hair was a shiny jet black, thick and straight. Her skin was flawless. She was slim and had a quiet, oval face that she accentuated with a French roll or braid. She had good taste in clothes and wore them so as to call attention to her uplifted breasts and nicely turned hips. She wore little jewelry, but knew how to wear it in the manner that less is more. Her nails were always manicured. She carried herself well and looked like someone used to living well. And she had lived well—at least during her five-year marriage.

Her parents were delighted and her friends envious to see her marry a successful Chinese businessman who owned and operated an investment firm. She and her husband drove expensive cars and lived in one of the first million-dollar tract homes in the area. They had become American citizens. They took frequent trips to Europe and Asia and did it first cabin always. They donated trips as prizes for fund-raisers. Their friends said admiringly that the local school board or Chamber of Commerce could use a man like Diana's husband. They threw parties. They lived the good life in America.

It was good for the five years. Then one day her husband didn't come home. She didn't call the sheriff's office right away because his colleagues displayed no real concern and hinted that she would hear from him soon enough.

Several days later, he called her from Geneva. He was sorry he had to leave without telling her in person, but a major investment opportunity had presented itself. It was worth millions, he said, but he had to act immediately if he was to avoid losing a business opportunity worth lots of money. Oh, she didn't know he had left town? Damn, he had told his secretary to call her, but she must have misunderstood. He would have to talk to her. He expected to return home soon, but he couldn't give her an exact date.

The news stunned Diana and she said almost nothing to him. She didn't tell him that two postal inspectors had already stopped by their house looking for him. They had asked her where he was and she could truthfully tell them she didn't know. They asked her about her involvement in his business and she told them that it consisted of playing hostess when her husband entertained clients and friends. She knew nothing of the world of investments. They asked her about offshore bank accounts, but she knew nothing of them. They would say only that they were investigating mail fraud.

Her husband left her penniless. He emptied their bank accounts and cancelled their joint credit cards. She lost both the house and cars because she couldn't make the payments. She had to pawn her jewelry. Men in suits came with search warrants and looked into every drawer and closet of the house. They even lifted the rugs to look for a floor safe. They interviewed dozens of Asians who had lost money with her husband's firm.

The authorities found no reason to prosecute her and, if they had, she would have had to rely on a public defender. Her friends abandoned her. Worse, some of the victims of her husband's fraud called her to vent their rage over having been bilked by people they had regarded as trusted friends. Two confronted her in public and raged at her in Mandarin and English within earshot of other Chinese. The final humiliation occurred when the men in suits had held a press conference and described her husband as an indicted fugitive, and insinuated that he might also have had a hidden ownership in a prostitution ring that catered to Asians and specialized in underage girls.

Diana became despondent, and then suicidal. She swallowed a bottle of pills one night in David's home when David and his wife were out. Fortunately, David and Mei came home early and called paramedics who raced her to a local hospital where they saved her life.

Only David helped her. He took her in while she studied nursing. She, like her brother, had been a good student in her teen years. She had finished her studies in minimum time, got her RN license and then trained for surgical nursing. Her motive was employability, not altruism. Her license was portable. She had learned that she could make a dependable income working close to home, or, if she chose, in another city where no one knew of her shame and loss of face. Better yet, she would never again be dependent on a man for support.

With her license and her exposure to western ways, Diana had become just too Americanized and too independent to play the role of wife to a man still steeped in the old ways and expectations. She made no secret of the fact that she had come to prefer

American men. She felt isolated from Asians and avoided social contact with them. Like so many professional women once married and once divorced, she wasn't sure if she would ever remarry. Her weekend flings with Gil, however, did much to satisfy both in their shared needs for intimacy and companionship.

She once told Gil that many Chinese wives were content to ignore their husbands' philandering or shady business dealings so long as they were paying the bills. Diana, however, had never bought into that. "I've come to have no respect for women who will hang on to a man as a meal ticket if they can afford otherwise," was the way she had put it.

When she married, she adopted the Western custom of taking her husband's family name, but after her divorce, she retained her maiden name so as to sever even the ceremonial tie to the man who had betrayed her. And, as if to distance herself even further from her Asian roots, she had plastic surgery on her eyes to make them "rounder."

She once laughed uproariously when Gil told her that she confirmed what he had always suspected: that the meek and mild Asian woman was a myth and that, in fact, any one of them would cut a man's balls off if he crossed her.

Gil never took Diana's affections for granted. He saw them as a gift. He was a basket case before her. For some time following his wife's death, Gil thought himself impervious to death because he was already dead. Diana's love had transformed him after losing a wife he had loved for so long.

Diana had given him a second chance at life, and she knew it. She knew it by the notes, flowers, and small gifts—a book, a CD, a gold bauble—which he regularly gave her.

Her ex-husband never did understand that even a new car and credit card couldn't substitute for little shows of attention. Better yet, Diana liked this man who made her laugh. And even better, he taught her how to enjoy her body.

Out of respect for her grief, Gil had not tried to see Diana since David's funeral. He sensed that she still had a sense of unreality over David's death, just as he did.

Finally, it was she who phoned Gil. "I know you mean well, but you don't have to hide from me. Why don't you think about coming over? I could use the company. If I were advising someone else, I'd tell them to stay around people at a time like this."

"Frankly, Diana, I was hoping to talk to you about your brother David."

His business-like tone put her off and she met it with humor. She affected a pidgin accent. "Oh, just talkee beezness? No buy me drink?" She chuckled at her own schoolgirl humor and giddiness, which she knew was a reaction and release of the emotion she had been bottling up.

Gil changed his tone. "Sweet, it struck me I know nothing of David's—or your—life before you came to the U.S. Maybe there's nothing to know, but I'd feel better if we talked about your life in China before you and David got here. How about tomorrow night? Can I buy you dinner someplace—your choice?"

"Sure, Gil, but let's eat here. I've got fresh fish and beef in the refrigerator. Take your pick. Bring a bottle of wine—something better than the rat poison you buy by the jug—and you can play barbecue chef. Oh yes, I bought a CD you haven't heard yet. See you tomorrow night, guy."

The next morning Gil was having coffee and a bagel in his favorite donut shop when he saw the story on the front page of the *Trib*. "Suspect Recants in Temple Murder," read the headline. The nineteen-year old said his confession was coerced and he had recanted it. The DA insisted he had a valid confession and balked at dropping the murder charge. The defendant's attorney—whom Gil knew to be a deputy public defender—took action to get the confession thrown out. The story quoted her as saying that she would file a Motion to Exclude. If that failed, she said, she would argue at trial that the confession was extracted under duress and didn't match other facts. Moreover, a psychologist who was an expert in the phenomena of false confessions would testify. Her client was no Boy Scout, she said. He didn't pretend to be and would plead guilty to several carjackings, but she was convinced he never murdered anyone.

Gil didn't know what to make of the recantation. On the one hand, he felt no major surprise, but certainly felt no smugness over it either and displayed none when he called Hara. Hara was expecting otherwise.

"You called to gloat, didn't you?"

"No, Steve, I'm not one to gloat. It's against my religion, but in case this kid's confession turns out to be false, after all, then I plan to continue following a hunch on why and even how David was murdered. That said though, I admit I don't have all the evidence yet."

"It's out of my hands, now Gil. Dropping charges against that punk is now up to the DA and the courts."

"Steve, I'd like nothing better than to be comfortable in the belief that this kid really did do it. We'll all feel better, but there's things nagging me."

"So you say—you've been playing Rockford after I told you not to?"

"As I said, Steve, it's just a hunch. I have to talk to some people first if you don't mind. I'll let you know if I learn anything relevant. Promise."

The news of the recantation confounded Gil, in part at least because he knew he should have felt vindicated in his doubts about the confession in the first place.

He called Rudy at his office. "Rudy, Gil again. Thanks again for the credit checks on Heng. I owe you. Does Al Garcia still work with you."

"Yeah, he's sitting right here."

"I only met him once. Is he the retired homicide detective? LAPD as I recall?"

"One and the same."

"Could you put him on, please?"

"This is Al."

"Al, Gil Rodrigues. Help me out, please. The Chang case—he was a long-time friend of mine. What's a body to make of that punk's recantation?"

"Gil, I probably wouldn't say this if I were still on the force, but false confessions do happen and it's not because we beat these guys. Sometimes they're retarded, tired or just plain stupid. Then they confess to something they didn't do—or, maybe a confederate did it and they take the rap out of some warped sense of loyalty or manliness. Dumb as it sounds, it happens, especially in that gang culture. But … "

"I'm all ears, Al. What's the 'but' part?"

"Nine times out of ten, recantations themselves are phony. The perp confesses to something he really did. Then, they put him back in with all the other jailhouse lawyers. They know it all. That's why they're in jail, too. They tell him not to worry about his confession. You know, 'Hey, homeboy, just recant. Tell 'em you confessed because you were scared and stick with the story'."

"And you've seen this while you were on the force?"

"Happens all the time, but they're usually not high-profile cases like this so you don't hear about them. If you want my opinion, I think this Romero iced your friend when he resisted."

"You're that confident, Al?"

"These guys rob, kill, rape and run from the cops on impulse. They confess on impulse, too. Then they recant on impulse—all to buy some time and muddy the water. This one, though, was smart enough wear gloves and get rid of the gun in a sewer."

Gil was silent, but Al knew he was still there.

When Gil did speak, his tone was subdued. It was the disquiet that comes with learning that one has been naïve or manipulated.

"Thanks, Al. You, Rudy and I have to meet for drinks soon."

After his talk with Garcia, Gil's own impulse was to call Sabrina, her mom and Diana and tell them he regarded the matter as closed; that Romero had, in fact, done it. The recantation, and not the confession, was phony. Case closed. But he resisted that impulse. To be sure, Romero wasn't going anywhere, and too many uncertainties were still bothering Gil. At a minimum, he wanted to talk with Diana before giving up on trying to find David's killer.

CHAPTER FIFTEEN

Gil always prepared for a date with Diana with some measure of self-consciousness. He couldn't help but be amused at how full-grown adults, himself included, became love-struck kids all over again when resuming the mating ritual. He knew he would stay at her place so he wore chinos and a polo shirt. He had never worn cologne, but he wore it now, because she had bought it for him. He brought his toothbrush and a change of underwear. A man's got to have a toothbrush and clean underwear when he visits a lady.

In his car, he passed the shops and stores where his late wife had liked to shop. He passed the restaurants where she and he had liked to eat. These places would always remind him of her. There was a time when even inanimate objects associated with her could send him into a blue funk. That finally had begun to change as he had gradually gotten used to living without someone he had loved for so long.

Gil picked up flowers, wine and a baguette. At Diana's place, he blended two margaritas and they sat on her kitchen stools and sipped them. Neither mentioned the recantation. Each sensed that any talk of it would be fruitless.

The drink made her garrulous. He listened patiently, occasionally leaning forward to kiss her on the cheek or forehead so as not to interrupt her. He was practiced and had learned long ago when to frown, when to smile and when to ask, "You're kidding?"

Yes, Diana had had her hands full earlier that day when a careless anesthesiologist had nearly lost a seven-year-old whose trachea had gone into spasm while he was still under. She had learned to anticipate such things and that had made her a good surgical nurse. She had already grabbed the inhalation aerosol and was ready to deliver it into the breathing tube even before the anesthesiologist had ordered her to do so. Gil told her it was called "grace under fire" and was a quality much admired.

After the margaritas, Gil grilled the beef on her patio barbecue while she made the salad and garlic bread. They washed it all down with a reserve Chianti that met her approval. Diana had slipped into a man's UCLA tee shirt that had once belonged to Gil, some fancy panties, and athletic socks. Except for a dab of perfume between her breasts this evening, it was her standard lounging dress with or without Gil's company. Tonight, however, she could see Gil might be too preoccupied for sex. With her appetite, which had come to exceed Gil's, she might be inclined to change the focus of his attention before morning. First, however, she had to let him satisfy his curiosities about David, which had brought him to her home seeking information.

After dinner, she poured two snifters of Grand Marnier straight up with water chasers and set them on cocktail napkins on the coffee table in front of the couch. She sat next to Gil with her knees pulled up and just touching Gil's thigh. Handing Gil his glass, she leaned forward, kissed him on the cheek, took a sip of her drink and then kissed him lightly on the lips so that he could taste the drop of the liqueur still on hers.

She held her snifter balanced on her thigh. "You won't find any dark secrets that I know of, Gil. What is it you want to know about David and me before we came here?"

"Tell me what you know about how David got his job with DaleeAhn."

"It's kind of the standard Chinese way, I guess. Nothing extraordinary."

"Standard how?"

"My Mandarin is fading. I speak so little of it these days, but the Chinese speak of '*guanxi.*' In English we'd say 'connections,' but *guanxi* is more than just connections or networking."

Gil added, "Blood relationships, schoolmates, childhood chums—those kinds of things?"

"Yes. It's a personal loyalty that underlies almost all business among Chinese."

"And David's *guanxi?* You and he don't seem to have a lot of blood ties here in the States."

"Our uncle is a Party member in China. He's wired to the old boy network there—or what's left of it. He's a VP of China Overseas Investments, the parent company of DaleeAhn."

Gil sipped his drink. "Makes sense now. David's bosses would have to hire David sight unseen when they set up shop here with their joint venture."

"Well, even if David weren't around, they would never hire a *gweilo*—a 'foreign devil'. No *guanxi* there." She changed to a half-sitting position and threw her calves over Gil's lap. "Earn your keep. Do my feet."

He stroked the tops of her thighs and shins lightly. Occasionally, he pressed his thumb between the balls of her feet, eliciting sighs from her when he did so. "So your uncle met a family obligation, and placed a loyal family member in a position to look after the money at the same time."

"David didn't discuss his day-to-day job responsibilities, but I'm certain he felt a stronger loyalty to his uncle than to Ming and his circle of friends. That's just our way. That's *guanxi*, even though David seemed to hate Ming and the other principals."

"And they him?"

"Apparently so. When I think about it, nobody liked those

guys including Mei, Sabrina, that Mr. Tillman, and me, too. There was some underlying creepiness about them that I can't put my finger on."

"So you've met Tillman as well as David's bosses?"

"Yes, they loved to throw expensive dinners and sometimes David dragged me to them. Then they'd get so obnoxiously drunk; nobody wanted to go to another. Sabrina really hated them."

"So I gathered. Ever meet the guy from the Chinese consulate?"

"Quon? Yes, very urbane—and handsome. He even asked me out. He seemed to be some kind of friend of our uncle in China. How close they were, I don't know, but they definitely knew each other."

"What can your woman's intuition tell me about Quon and Ming?"

"Aren't you going to ask if I went out with Quon?"

"I don't want to know. I just hope you keep only one lover at a time. Answer my question." He tickled her sole so that she jumped reflexively.

"Since you ask, he and Ming did seem to share some kind of bond. The way they laughed—that sort of thing."

"More *guanxi*, I guess?"

"Definitely. More *guanxi*."

Gil took another sip of his drink and placed it back on the table. He stopped stroking her legs and looked at her. "Diana, I want your cold-blooded opinion. If you can put aside the fact that David was your brother, do you think he'd steal from the company?"

"My cold-blooded opinion? The common belief among the Chinese here—true or not—is that these joint ventures with Chinese companies are a license to steal."

"Ever hear of any of them getting caught at it?"

"Not directly," she said. "Although stories pop up in the Chinese press and community now and then about someone getting caught and getting shot."

"So the word among the Chinese is that it's a way to get money out of China and into their pockets even with the risk of getting shot for it? How about David himself? I always considered your brother to be scrupulously honest, but do you think he might have been taking anything from the till?"

Diana paused, placed a throw pillow under her head and looked at the ceiling. "All of us have 20-20 hindsight. Then I think of odd comments David made about his job. At the time they didn't mean anything special, but looking back, I have to wonder."

"What was the substance of these comments?"

"And that's all I remember—the substance, but he seemed to imply he didn't like how Ming and his associates were running things. He had been hoping for some long-term employment, but he couldn't see it the way things were."

"Did David ever mention money—his pay, his share?"

"Again, he would imply that his bosses were getting a big piece of the pie, while he worked for crumbs off the table, but he never elaborated as I remember. Frankly, I sensed some level of envy."

"His bosses with the new cars, expensive dinners, and credit cards? And his uncle getting him the job implied, to David at least, that he should share in the spoils?"

"Yes, it had to have caused some level of resentment in him. You know—why couldn't he have a company car or corporate credit card like they did?"

"And, knowing David's reserve, he was afraid to articulate it too openly lest he compromise himself or jeopardize his job. But … " Gil paused. "He just had to call his uncle in China to spoil their fun."

"Exactly, but by the same token, he'd be out of a job if the company had closed."

"Any idea if he ever made that call?"

"No, and if he did, I doubt he'd tell me."

She kicked her legs abruptly to the floor and nearly jumped to a kneeling position on the couch next to Gil. She threw her arms around Gil's neck and nibbled his earlobe, sending a small shiver through him. With her arms still around his neck she murmured into his ear, "This interrogation isn't much fun. Aren't you supposed to strip search me now and make me confess to stealing pencils from the hospital?" She pulled away slightly and playfully drew her tee shirt up to expose her navel and midriff.

Gil suppressed a smile and pulled her tee shirt down in feigned indignation. "Behave yourself. I don't recall that getting your clothes off requires a lot of effort. Besides, we'd need the Library of Congress to hold your confessions."

"Are you trying to ruin my reputation as a celibate Florence Nightingale?"

"Celibate? About as celibate as a doe bunny. I think you're a succubus."

"Is that some big history-major word? Sounds sexy."

"It is. She's a mediaeval demon who comes to men in their sleep and screws them to death."

"Where did you pick that up?"

"I learned it in a trashy historical novel I read in high school. Don't recall the title, but it had lots of rape and pillage—oh, and maidens being carried off by feudal lords on their wedding nights. Heady stuff for a 15-year-old who had never been laid."

"You poor baby, but I definitely qualify for the succubus job. How do I audition?" She hopped back to her knees on the couch next to him and again locked her arms around his neck. Gil tried to look solemn, but she saw the half-smile she evoked.

She continued the teasing. "Tell me about all those little Vietnamese chicks you did when you were there."

Gil did a mock British accent. "A gentleman does not kiss and tell. Some things a man takes to his grave, my dear. Mustn't earn the white feather, you know."

"You're no fun."

"Okay, milady, if it turns you on, they were all virgins. Their pimps guaranteed it."

She chuckled and pretended to be aroused by the statement. "Umm, sounds exciting. All virgins, eh?"

"Come here," he said softly. He reached around her waist and pulled her against his chest so that he could feel her breasts against his shirt and skin. Her closeness and the thinness of the tee shirt made it obvious that she wore no bra as usual.

She whispered, "I love the way you hold me."

"I'm glad you weren't raised a good Catholic girl."

"How's that? Wait. Don't tell me. Because I'm easy?"

"Well, yes, you're definitely an easy lay—at least with me—but the good Catholic girls where I come from mostly had little mustaches and hairy legs that their mothers—or nuns—wouldn't let them shave. Only wanton hussies did that."

"And you like 'em wanton, don't you? No sir, no Newark, New Joisey girls allowed." She kissed him lightly on the lips, flicking her tongue ever so quickly as she did so. Once more, he tasted the liqueur on her tongue.

Gil nearly leapt to his feet, picking Diana up at the same time. "God help me. I adore you. You're the sweetest thing that's happened to me since ... " He paused.

"Since you lost Helen?" She looked straight into his eyes. "Don't be afraid to say it. You loved her. It's obvious, but she's gone. My husband's gone, we're still alive and you're the nicest thing that's happened to me, too, since I quit playing sap to that sonofabitch."

He started toward her bedroom and she clung to him with her arms still around his neck. She teased, "Did I hear you say

God help you? And aren't you an atheist? Why would God want to help a rogue like you anyway?"

Gil laughed. "I don't know why I said that. I probably heard it in a movie, because I certainly don't watch soap operas."

When he reached the bed, he swung her as if he was going to throw her on the bed. She gasped and clung harder to his neck. He set her down gently and nuzzled her neck, breasts and midriff in a way that he found tickled her. Laughing and giggling like a child, she pushed hard and explosively against his chest. He rolled on his back. She put her head on his shoulder and threw her thigh over his hips. She outlined his face and lips with her index finger. He took her hand and kissed the palm.

They caught their breaths. "What are you thinking?" she asked.

"Why does a woman always ask a man that at a time like this?" His voice conveyed mild annoyance.

She lowered her voice into a poor imitation of a gypsy fortuneteller. "Didn't you ever learn? We women have mystical powers. We can tell by his eyes if a man is lying."

"I believe it. And when we lie?"

"You're history."

"I want to know who killed your brother."

"I know that, lover-guy, but we're not going to find that out tonight. Aren't you going to take your clothes off?"

"Sounds like a plan," he said. He stood and threw his clothes over a chair. She pulled off her tee shirt and tossed it at Gil and giggled when it draped over his head and covered one eye. He pulled it off slowly and looked at her, as one would reproach a mischievous waif. It smelled of her perfume. The sight of her breasts took his breath away every time. Firm and perched high, they were in perfect proportion to her shoulders and looked as if they had been carved from white marble. The nipples were prominent, the aureoles wide and brown. He had told her more than once that her breasts belonged on a statue. She had fine hips and long, shapely thighs.

He pulled off her oversized socks one at a time and kissed her insteps as he did so. Her feet were always as well cared for as her hands. He dropped to his knees and grabbed her hips gently, feeling her hip bones with his thumbs as he did so, and he pulled her to the edge of the bed. He kissed her thighs. He kissed her belly and pubis. He kissed the creases where her thighs joined her torso. At first he always kissed everywhere but the special place. That could wait for now.

Never having carried life, her belly was flat. Diana never removed her panties right away because she loved to feel his breath and his touch through the material. He knew it because she reminded him every time they made love. He knew it by her response. She liked the tease, but couldn't tolerate it for long. Then she would quickly slip out of her panties, which signaled a now-urgent need for an escalation of his efforts to the special place that she had been only vaguely aware of before Gil. He was only the second man who had ever made love to her. It was that place that her husband either hadn't known about—or cared to know.

"Where are you sending me?" She always asked that same question at that moment, but he never replied.

And then, when he was over her, they clung to each other with entwined fingers, legs and mouths. They absorbed each other's sweat and each other's scent into their skins and into their nostrils as they came together as one. And, like all lovers at all times, they became the center of the universe each time they made love.

Then, when they were spent, they lay side by side. Afterwards, she always put her head on his shoulder, laid her hand on his chest and slipped into a half-sleep. Her head on his shoulder at that special moment represented an exquisite tenderness—a tenderness that healed all wounds, all grief, and all of the betrayals each of them had ever experienced.

In the morning, as Gil washed and dressed, Diana could see that he was preoccupied. She walked up behind him and put her arms around his waist. "What's on your mind, sailor? Your thoughts are going a mile a minute."

Gil turned, smiled, kissed her on the forehead and patted her behind as he did so. "Got to go. Got things to do and people to see. I'll keep you informed, love. Bye for now."

CHAPTER SIXTEEN

Years later, Gil would speak of this day as one of the worst in his life. It started routinely enough. He interviewed and took statements from three witnesses to an industrial accident for one of his insurance clients, after which he went back to his office to write up the interviews. On the way home, he stopped at the market for some food, liquor and household items. When he reached his house, he put the food away while he listened to his messages. There was one from Lieutenant Hara.

"Gil, this is Steve. It's about 3:30. Give me a call."

It was past five and Hara might be off duty, so Gil paged him in the hope he might have some news about David's murder. Hara called back immediately.

"Got some news, Steve?"

"It's news of sorts. Gil, you're pretty close with David's sister Diana, are you not?"

"Yes, I'd say 'close' about describes it, but you've known that for some time, so why ask? What's up?"

"I'm only fifteen minutes away. I'd like to stop by. Okay?"

"Of course, Steve." Gil grabbed a beer from the refrigerator. He had bought the "lite" type in the hope it would help keep off extra weight.

Hara arrived with Detective Chin. "You recall my lead man on the case?"

Gil acknowledged Chin and offered them drinks. They accepted ice water. All three sat at the dining room table.

"Some news, Steve?" Gil looked first at Hara, then at Chin for a response. Both men wore a solemn expression that Gil found unnerving.

"Something happen with Romero and his confession?"

Hara wouldn't look straight at Gil. He was almost mumbling.

"We regard the Chang murder case as still open."

"The DA backed off on the murder charge against Romero. Is that what you're going to tell me, Steve?"

The lieutenant still wouldn't look Gil in the eye. "His lawyer let him take a polygraph. It was inconclusive, but the DA dropped the murder charge on David, and Romero copped a plea on the other carjackings. He'll spend decades in jail on those charges alone, which include kidnapping."

"You could have told me this on the phone, Steve."

"There's something else we need to talk about." He finally began looking at Gil while he spoke. "We haven't spoken to Diana yet, but has she ever discussed her finances with you?"

"Frankly, no. Why would she? She seems to make an adequate income. That's my sense anyway."

"But you, on the other hand, struggle to pay the bills. Must be frustrating at times."

"Some months, yes, but where's this going, Steve?"

"You own any guns, Gil?"

"Haven't touched one, bought one, or owned one since leaving the Army. Never had a real need for one."

"Let me just lay it out, Gil. David owned a one-million-dollar life insurance policy. His wife and his sister Diana—your honey—were co-beneficiaries. Sabrina is only a contingent beneficiary. A half-million would generate—oh—I'd say, forty to fifty thousand per year invested smart, wouldn't you?"

Gil pushed away from the table. "Steve, you sonofabitch! You're saying that gives Diana and me a motive, which makes us both suspects?"

Hara was unfazed by Gil's response. "I am. You and she together had motive and you of all people, Gil, know how easy it is to hire a killer with the right connections. And, everyone in the local community knows she and her ex-spouse lived la dolce vita before he split for Switzerland one step ahead of the law."

"Steve, you're crazy!" Gil placed his hands on the table as if he were ready to stand. Chin laid his hand on the grip of his sidearm. Without taking his eyes off Chin for one second, Gil said, "Steve, tell junior here that if he pulls that piece on me, a surgeon will have to remove it from his colon."

Hara displayed no alarm, but just waved off Chin, who put his hands back on the table.

Gil continued, his voice now softer. "That kid's recantation bit you in the ass. So now you're trying to save face by grabbing at straws just to say you still have suspects."

Hara pressed on. "We just learned about the life insurance or you would have heard from me before. As for your sweetie, we can't find a paper trail connecting her to her former husband's scams, but the people he bilked believe she was up to her cute little ass in his business."

"She wasn't charged with anything, Steve." Gil's voice was now reaching normal levels.

"That might mean only that her husband was careful not to leave a paper trail with her tracks on it. That way, she wouldn't have to go down with him if the crap hit the fan."

"Steve, you make her out to be some kind of Dragon Lady pulling strings behind the scenes. She's not that kind of person. I know her."

"You know her in a Biblical sense, maybe, but Asian women have a way of closing their eyes to a husband's dealings as long as the guy is paying the bills."

"I'm not that naïve, Steve. She was nearly destroyed by her husband's scams and devastated by David's murder. And you know about the intense loyalty in Chinese families."

"Gil, I read the investigation files the feds have on her husband and his business. You would have no way of knowing this, but he kept some nasty types around for 'personal security'. I'm talking about Asian gang types, fully capable of carrying out a hit for the right price. Your honey could not have avoided meeting them and knowing how to contact one if she were so inclined."

Gil shook his head in disbelief. "Steve, this is crazy."

"Is it, Gil? I hope you're right, but more than a few times her husband had one of these characters chauffeur her around."

"What was she supposed to do—refuse the service?"

"Gil, just so you know how serious this could be—informers tell us one of these chauffeurs is a well-known hit man in Asian gang circles. One of these days we'll nail him and he'll be looking at the gas chamber, which is what you can get for murder-for-hire *if* you get my drift."

"Steve, I can't believe this is happening."

"The kind of daily contact in the privacy of a car can make for some friendly associations. She'd have plenty of opportunity to get cozy with a guy who'd kill for money as quick as you and I would swat a fly."

"It's unreal that you could can even *think* this way." Gil looked at Hara with an expression of total disbelief.

"Gil, ever read about the old Murder, Incorporated in places like Brooklyn back in the thirties? A lot of their business came from women looking to do away with husbands or relatives for insurance money. It's the oldest motive in the world."

"It's not her and it's not me. You blew it on the phony confession from the carjacker. You're blowing it with this theory, too." Gil's expression was now grim.

"As I said, old friend, I hope I'm wrong, but I have to think of these things. Frankly, I don't want to believe you'd be involved in anything like this, but I'm inclined to ask a judge for a search warrant for her bank records to see if she made any large cash withdrawals before David's murder."

"Steve, no one—not Sabrina, David's wife or sister—said a word to me about the insurance. Never heard of it until this moment. And all I know of her husband's scams and hirelings is what I read in the paper. This is all news to me."

"For your sake, Gil, I hope it is. But we'll be talking to your Diana. Right now, you and she are on my list of suspects, if only because you could have had motive. You know the routine. Don't go far. If you do, we may think you're running and may have something to hide."

Hara and Chin stood to leave. Gil spoke. "Steve, if you're serious about me and Diana as suspects, I suggest you do a polygraph on me. I can't speak for Diana."

"Okay, Gil, let me talk to the DA first. I'll get back to you on your offer. Oh—just a thought—if your sweetie has an alibi, then I hope you haven't been set up."

Gil glared at Hara for a long moment before speaking. Then coldly, "Get out of my house—now."

Gil knew that a perfectly innocent person could appear to be hiding something by doing something impulsive or by overreacting to a routine suspicion. He had to talk with Diana, but the last thing he wanted was a phone record of his calling her between the time Hara left his house and Hara's subsequent interview with her. A phone tap wasn't improbable, either; court orders were easy to obtain from a judge favorable to the prosecutor's side. His perfectly warranted curiosity about Hara's suspicion could easily appear as if Gil and she were collaborating on alibis. Gil's talk with Diana would wait until after Hara and Chin interviewed her. Gil had nothing to hide and he had to hope Diana had nothing to hide. In the meantime, he wanted to talk to Sabrina.

Gil reached Sabrina at her mother's home where she was still residing. "What do you know about life insurance on your dad?"

"I knew my dad had life insurance. That's all. Last night when that Detective Chin was here, my mom showed him the policy. That was when I learned that it has a substantial face value. Dad made Mom and my Aunt Diana the beneficiaries."

"That's a pretty hefty policy for a man of your dad's means, don't you think, honey?"

"I understand it was ten-year term insurance about to expire next month."

"I see. When he bought it, it had a cheap premium. That's typical of term insurance. He could afford it then."

"Yes," she said. "And frankly, I doubt if he could have afforded the same amount when it came up for renewal. I guess those insurance companies really raise the premiums as you get older. But what brought all this up, Unc?"

"Hara and Chin were here awhile ago. They seem to think that policy gave Diana and me and your mom, too, a motive."

Sabrina was silent for a full half-minute. When she spoke her voice quavered slightly. Gil heard her catch her breath. "Surely they can't be serious? My mom? Aunt Diana? You?"

"He wouldn't be doing his job if he didn't look for motive among family, friends, and colleagues. I'm sure he wouldn't want to believe that any more than you would, honey, but motive often points the way. But then he has to find means and opportunity."

"I don't even know when my mom and Aunt Diana will get the money. I'm sure there's some kind of paperwork, but it must be routine with people dying every day."

"This is my area, honey. Yes, it's normally routine, but if the insurance company gets any idea that the beneficiaries may have murdered the policyholder, they'll drag their feet on payment until the police either catch the real perpetrator or rule out the beneficiaries as suspects."

"Aunt Diana has a job and it pays well. My mom hasn't held a job in years and her English is limited. She'll need that money to live on."

"Yes, a half-million should be a nice little income to supplement her widow's social security. She'll need that money to live on, but I don't need a cop and a good friend thinking that I, and a lady I think the world of, might be accessories to the murder of a friend."

Gil waited until the following day to visit Diana. He timed his visit so that he would arrive shortly after she would normally arrive home from work. He hadn't wanted to call first so she wasn't expecting him. He heard her ask, "Who's there?" from behind her locked "security" door.

"It's Gil, Diana. Let me in, please."

She was still wearing street clothes. "I think I know why you're here." They had always exchanged a quick peck on the lips, but didn't do so this time. The tension was obvious to both of them.

"I hope not. Has Lieutenant Hara or Detective Chin talked with you yet?"

"Yes, they interviewed me at work today during my lunch break. They didn't come right out and say it, but they seem to think that I and maybe you and my sister-in-law had good reason to kill David."

"Do we?"

"Gil, I didn't know whether to laugh or cry at that question. I was suicidal when David took me in after my husband ... oh, that bastard!" She pursed her lips and her eyes filled. She composed herself and continued. "Well, you know the rest. I couldn't imagine hurting David for all the money in the world."

"My gut says that's the truth, but I had to hear you say it to my face. Want me to go now?"

She shook her head in a silent No. Then she said, "Stay awhile. Make us a couple of margaritas while I change. I could use a drink."

Gil blended the drinks and poured them. A few moments

later, Diana arrived in the kitchen wearing her after-work dress of tee shirt and athletic socks. Today she wore sweatpants.

They sat on barstools in her kitchen, sipping their drinks. Both were silent and did not look at each other for several minutes. Finally Gil spoke. "How much did you know about your husband and his dealings?"

"I never knew any details until the postal inspectors and other government types started asking questions. A few weeks before he left the country, I began to suspect that he was running some kind of scam, but I truly didn't know what kind. I just kept my fingers crossed that it wouldn't blow up in his face."

"What kinds of things tipped you off?"

"His clients would find our unlisted home number somehow. I'd hear him telling them they had to be patient, that sometimes these investments took longer than expected—that sort of thing. He began getting more and more of those calls and, the more he got, the more he drank and smoked and the later he stayed out."

"Steve Hara said your husband hired bodyguards who weren't listed in the Yellow Pages."

"He said it was just a precaution—that he and I weren't in any real danger. He said that there was always the risk of some disgruntled investor blaming his advisor for losses. And yes, I let my husband have one of these creeps drive me around at times. It was easier than arguing with him about it."

"So your husband was running a Ponzi scheme and the chickens were coming home to roost."

"I never heard of a Ponzi scheme until those government guys started coming around, but I learned fast that whatever it was my husband was doing, it was illegal."

"When did you learn about David's life insurance?"

"Almost from the day he bought it, about nine years ago. He was quite proud of his purchase and told me and Mei that we were co-beneficiaries."

"Why would he make you a co-beneficiary and not a contingent beneficiary like Sabrina? Or is that just more *guanxi?*"

"That's exactly what it was, Gil. He wanted his wife and sister taken care of first and then Sabrina in case something happened to us. Sabrina has an education and her whole life ahead of her."

"Did your husband ever discuss his business with David?"

"They had casual talks as I recall. Why do you ask?"

"Just curious. And your bodyguards—did you ever talk to any of them after your husband took off for Geneva?"

"No—I wouldn't have known where to find one of them if I had wanted to. Gil, I'm worried."

"How so?"

"Hara—he's poisoned it between us—hasn't he? There's a tension here tonight between us—a tension we've never had before."

"Sweet … " Gil paused and then looked down and away from her before bringing his eyes back to meet hers. "I've had this feeling for some time now that David was murdered because of what he knew. If I'm right, then maybe that kid's recantation is real after all."

"What kinds of things did my brother know?"

"I don't mean to be vague or mysterious. I just can't fill you in on that right now. One reason I can't is because I now know things, too—things that could get me in trouble for not disclosing them to the law—not to mention how I found them out. I shouldn't even be saying this much to you."

"I won't press. You're not staying tonight?"

"No, not tonight, sweet, but I'll make it up to you. Promise. I've got to think. I've got homework to do and people to see." Gil drained the few sips left in his glass, kissed Diana and left.

Gil had limited himself to the one drink at Diana's place. He had to stay focused now. He had raised the stakes with his initially tentative and then bold plunge into David's murder case. Diana's and his livelihood and maybe even their freedom were now in jeopardy. If it was discovered that he had broken into DaleeAhn, he could go to jail. He could be prosecuted for withholding evidence.

In a worst-case scenario, it would mean felony convictions for both Diana and him. It was nightmarish. He and his lover were now suspects in a capital murder case. There was no credible evidence—even circumstantial—to link either of them to the murder, but Gil knew that people had been indicted, even convicted, of murder on little or no substantive evidence.

Anyone who read the paper knew that this was by no means a rare occurrence. Police and prosecutors under pressure to "do something," need only persuade themselves that they have the right person or persons, after which they focus all their energies on convicting those suspects.

After that, the DA would drag the suspects before a grand jury for an indictment. The joke about grand juries is that they will indict a ham sandwich. With an indictment in hand, the prosecutor needs only the "right" jury—one whose members think that it's their job to deliver a guilty verdict in the misguided belief that the defendants must have "done something" to appear in court in the first place.

Gil had been home alone the night of David's murder, but he knew of no way to prove that. He hadn't even used the phone. Diana had been at work. Gil believed he could survive prison, but the mere thought of Diana being under suspicion made him ill. If Gil were indicted, he would lose his house to pay for bail, and for lawyers to defend both himself and Diana because neither of them had the cash necessary to pay for a competent defense.

He knew it would take some time, if ever, to forgive Hara for believing that he would ever commit murder for profit or that Diana could ever murder her brother, a brother who had given her back her life.

Now more than ever, Gil needed to start testing his theory of David's murder, and he believed he knew just the man to help him. The following day he would drop in on Jack.

CHAPTER SEVENTEEN

It had taken long time and a lot of pain for Gil to learn not to dredge up things from long ago. Some people liked to wallow in the past, but that was an indulgence Gil could no longer afford. It made a man blue. It made a man drink.

That day, however, he couldn't stop one memory from surging up and washing over him. He couldn't stop it because he was on his way to see Jack Corbett, and, as always, the freeway ride made him pensive. It was Jack who had kept Gil out of a military prison at the cost of his own Army career—something Gil had learned years after the event. A man doesn't forget a friend like Jack.

It had happened in 1961 in another life half a world away. Gil was Sergeant Rodrigues then, and stationed in Korea, when he heard the news that JFK was sending 100 Special Forces troops—"trained for guerilla warfare" in news parlance—to Vietnam. At that time, that news had no special significance for Gil. He knew little more about such men than did the general public. The Special Forces public relations people painted them as men trained in derring-do warfare who got to wear their rakish green berets only after JFK signed an executive order authorizing the headgear.

The news of their assignment to Vietnam had become significant to Gil when his unit asked for volunteers willing to go to Vietnam to support those Special Forces. The Special Forces needed intelligence support and the South Vietnamese troops needed training in modern intelligence-gathering methods.

Gil was bored in Korea, but he had seven months to go on his tour. Vietnam tours were largely voluntary then and it was possible to sign on for a mere six-month tour. And, for someone who was twenty-four, Vietnam sounded like a cool mission for one's resume. That bravado would have its price.

Sergeant Gil Rodrigues was a spook. Put simply, his unit listened in on enemy communications. They analyzed radio traffic and broke ciphers and did radio direction finding, all to guess an enemy's intentions or location. Three out of four of the enlisted men in his detachment had at least four years of college. What was called "signals intelligence" or SIGINT in the first two world wars was now called "communications intelligence" or COMINT in the acronymic world of the military. Like all spooks, Gil and his buddies worked in anonymity, their successes unheralded.

Once in Vietnam, Gil and his men put their uniforms back on while "in the field," which translated as assignments to "radio research" detachments in the Special Forces camp at Hoa Cam in Quang Nam Province. The very nature of their work brought them so close to the enemy that casualties in units like Gil's were among the highest of any support groups.

Gil and his men managed to earn a measure of real, if grudging, respect from the Berets when they left their desks and took their equipment into the bush and put their lives at risk, gathering intelligence that could save others' lives.

The rules dictated that any mission requiring a trip into enemy territory be assigned, whenever possible, to South Vietnamese soldiers. To lose an ARVN soldier wouldn't cause a ripple in the American press. The goal was to prevent American boys from getting killed at all costs.

Gil found it hard to tolerate the ill-concealed contempt of the Green Berets for support people. That drove Gil to plant—on his own—listening devices along trails used by the enemy miles from his camp. In doing so, he carried only a light hammock, one day's food and water, a compass and a sidearm. If discovered, he would take as many of the enemy down with him as he could, but he would take his own life to avoid capture.

That plan arose from fear, not courage; Gil was just too steeped in the history of modern warfare. The mere thought of spending weeks or months being beaten or tortured made his stomach churn and his legs turn to rubber. He pledged to die first.

Gil managed to plant four listening devices and spent ten nights in the bush by himself in so doing before his superiors put a stop to it. He didn't believe any colonels cared about his welfare; they just didn't want any bad press.

The civilian from Utah arrived at Gil's camp several weeks after Gil himself. The man never identified himself as CIA, but it didn't take long for everyone to figure out that that was exactly what he was. Tom Loman was clearly ex-military, a man used to giving orders. He was only slightly shorter than Gil's 6'2". His skin was fair but freckled, with the kind of wrinkles one sees in the faces of ranchers. His hair was rust colored, but kinky. He looked like a man who kept himself in shape. Gil guessed he was in his early forties. He spoke with a drawl, a drawl that he switched on and off as it suited the situation. Gil never saw him smoke and the story among the enlisted men was that he drank only Dr. Pepper in the Officers' Club.

Loman's plan was simple and, on the surface at least, it had a lot of precedent. He would have the Special Forces train small groups of South Vietnamese soldiers in guerilla warfare techniques and then have them dropped into areas controlled by the Communists. "Fightin' fire with fire," Loman would say time and again in his affected Texas drawl. He called it "Operation Poison Pill."

Captain Jack Corbett and his men had been given only four weeks to train the first two groups. "They already know basic soldiering," Loman would say. "You guys teach 'em the sneaky stuff they need to know." The groups were all volunteers, fiercely anticommunist and loyal to the South. Their officers and non-coms were well educated. A few had attended school in the U.S. Most trusted their American mentors and were eager to take the fight to an enemy they hated.

Even Gil and his men had played a part. They taught the volunteers radio security techniques and what to do if they took a command post and stumbled on to enemy maps, rosters, radio logs or codebooks. They were to photograph any documents they found with cameras provided for the purpose and then leave those documents where they found them in the hope that the enemy wouldn't realize that the documents had been copied by hostile forces.

Men form bonds quickly in wartime. Shared drinks in a bar or brothel, a brawl with members of another service, but most of all—a collective sense of shared danger—become the glue of friendships. Only on rare occasions do those friendships last a lifetime, but, for their duration, they are as strong and as intense as any other.

Sergeant Duc "Duke" Tran and Gil became friends. Tran, Vietnamese by birth, had spent two years at Cal State. He returned to Vietnam when his parents could no longer support him and his education in the U.S. He had a wife and two small kids. His hope was to see an end to the conflict with the North and to resume a conventional life in his parents' business in Saigon. Gil and Duke regarded themselves as civilians in uniform.

When the training of the guerilla units had been nearly completed, Loman held closed-door sessions with the groups with only an interpreter to assist. He referred to the sessions as "big-picture briefings on information that members of the units would have to know to be motivated and fully effective." Why a man like Loman lapsed into bureaucratic lingo to describe this task would become apparent to Gil only days after Sergeant Tran's group had been dropped into enemy-held territory.

On day one, the men of "Operation Poison Pill" sent a radio message indicating that they were safely inside enemy territory. They were to send reports every twenty-four hours, but nothing was heard for the next four days. On day six, Tran's group sent a message with a "misspelling" of a word in the text. That misspelling was a doubling code only Gil's men knew. It meant that Tran and his group had been captured and were being forced to send radio messages to appear as if everything was normal. That all subsequent radio traffic from the group contained no significant information and always contained the "misspelling" simply reconfirmed that the men had been captured.

When Gil reported the probable capture to Loman and Captain Corbett, Loman had registered no surprise or frustration. He offered only a cryptic smile. Gil and the captain exchanged looks. Jack spoke first. "Is there something we should know, Tom?"

Loman made a thumbs-up sign. "I'll brief you all shortly on a need-to-know basis, of course. You've both done a great job, but there's a Phase Two in this operation and you and Sergeant Rodrigues will play a critical role in this phase. We'll need to know if it's working the way we hope it will."

"If what's working?" Jack asked.

Loman's tone was that of someone standing at a lectern. "It's not enough to get an enemy to believe false information. He's got to act on it."

Gil and Captain Corbett said nothing, but just stared at Loman's back as he left Jack's hut. Gil put his face into his hands and spoke with his face covered. "You know, Captain, guys like Loman get commendations and promotions for doing things like this. Take some men who just want to defend their country. Fill them full of phony information you want the enemy to believe and dump them where they'll get captured and tortured."

Jack shook his head. "Let's hope there's more to this."

"Will you get a commendation, too, Captain, for this diabolical hoax? And what kinds of bastards sitting at desks in Virginia approve these things?"

"I'll pretend I didn't hear that, Sergeant. Let's you and I hope we don't have all the facts, because if we do, I may shoot the son of a bitch before you do. Remember, my people trained those men. You're dismissed—and stay away from that asshole."

Loman and his people occupied the second floor of a cinder block building that had been a school. Maybe, if on the way back to his desk, Gil hadn't spotted Loman climbing the stairs to his office things would have been different.

"Tom?—Mr. Loman?" Gil was at the foot of the stairs and Loman had reached the top. Loman said nothing, but stopped and waited for Gil to reach him.

"What can I do for you, Sergeant?"

When Gil reached Loman, he stood almost in Loman's face. "Where do they make people like you or are you just born bastards?"

Loman's tone was patronizing. "You're still young, Sergeant. You've got a lot to learn about how wars are conducted. Stick around. Maybe you'll learn something."

"I'm all for screwing the enemy in any way we can, but this takes the cake. What if the press learned about it?"

"Is that a threat, Sergeant, because if it is, you'll find yourself facing a court martial." Loman tapped Gil's chest. The adrenaline kicked in. Gil felt it in his gut.

"If I go to jail, it won't be for just making a threat. You delivered a dozen good men into the hands of torturers as callously as some people drown a bag of puppies. Your bosses at Langley must think you're one clever bastard. One of those men you shipped off to hell was a friend of mine."

Loman's expression was one of contempt. "Was he really now, Sergeant? Oh? A gook with a college education? Were you sucking each other's cocks out behind the latrine or was it all in the ass? Don't all you Portugees take it in the ass?"

"Not all of us, asshole. No sir, not all of us." With that, Gil grabbed Loman's shirt by the shoulder seams. He jerked Loman's shoulders to the right while kicking his ankles to the left. Loman tried to hold on to Gil's wrists and to break the hold, but Gil's movements were too explosive and Loman found himself heading off into space in an uncontrolled, headfirst tumble down the concrete stairs.

Loman's expression registered hatred and shock. He kept a rolling eye contact with Gil as he tumbled head over heels. Gil ran down the steps after Loman even before his victim managed to break his fall two treads from the bottom. Loman's hands, elbows and the left side of his face were abraded and bleeding from contact with the concrete stairs. His gasping suggested broken ribs and his face had turned pale.

Gil reached Loman only a moment after he had stopped tumbling and once more grabbed him by the shoulder seams. He pulled the man's face inches from his own. "You'd better thank the reptile you pray to that I haven't cut off your balls and stuffed them down your throat. Oh, and by the way, you little redneck, don't ever call me a queer again."

They didn't formally arrest Gil; he was confined to base and was to report to the orderly room every two hours while he awaited his court-martial. Loman would testify that Gil had attacked him without provocation. What Gil said wouldn't matter. The whole thing would be over in thirty minutes, after which Gil would be taken off to prison in handcuffs. Enlisted men just weren't allowed to attack officers or civilian government employees without paying the price. Had Gil been a soldier at the turn of the century, he might have been shot.

After ten days of restriction to base and two hours before Gil's court-martial, the company clerk caught up with Gil. "Sergeant major wants you now."

The sergeant major made Gil stand at attention for a good three minutes while he looked at papers on his desk. One of Gil's own men wearing a sidearm was standing there. Gil was beyond intimidation if only because he was resigned to whatever they were going to do to him. More than that, he had now come to hate people like Loman and the sergeant major more than ever.

Finally the sergeant major addressed Gil. "Just who do you know?"

"Sar-major?"

"A congressman? A senator? The president? Who-in-hell-do-you-know?"

"I swear I don't know what you're talking about, Sar-major."

"Well, somebody up there must like you, but it breaks my heart that your court martial is off. Guys like you—you think you're better than everybody else—you belong in jail. What you've pulled here I haven't figured out yet, but here are your orders. You've got thirty minutes to pack your gear. Corporal Moore will be with you every step of the way until your plane leaves with you on it. You're going back to Korea to finish out your enlistment."

Gil was in a state of disbelief. "I'd be lying if I said that wasn't good news, Sar-major, but I swear I don't know what's going on here."

"In any event, Sergeant, don't plan on a career in the Army. The word on troublemakers like you spreads real fast. Now get the hell out of my sight."

Fifteen years would pass before Gil learned it was Captain Jack Corbett who had kept him out of prison for his assault on the rancher from Utah who didn't smoke or drink.

CHAPTER EIGHTEEN

As Gil pulled into the parking lot of Jack's office building, he recalled the first time he had seen him again, fifteen years after Vietnam. Jack was a civilian, only recently retired from the CIA, which he had joined when his Army career had stalled. It was only then and over drinks that Gil learned that it was Jack who had saved him by calling in an IOU from an Associated Press reporter. The reporter had never filed the story, but he knew what buttons to push with Jack's superiors: "Would the general please comment on rumors about the 'sacrifice' of a South Vietnamese insertion team as a means of feeding false information to the enemy?" Jack's commanding officer and Loman got the message and put their own careers ahead of any pleasure they might take in sending some smart-ass buck sergeant like Gil Rodrigues to prison.

"After that," Jack said to Gil, "my fitness rating went into the toilet. I'd never see a major's leaf, but the CIA was hiring ex-Special Forces by the busload then, so at least I've got a pension."

"I feel I owe you an apology of some sort. For years, I didn't know who to thank. I'm sorry."

Jack shrugged. "You owe me nothing. If you hadn't busted Loman's ribs, I might have shot the sonofabitch myself. For a while there, I gave serious thought about taking him into the bush and making him disappear. I was surprised you didn't shoot him outright."

"I almost did. I was wearing a .45 at the time. But, I should have taken the fall, not you."

"Gil, you and I did what we thought we had to do at the time. We stood up to someone or something and paid the price. Unfortunately nobody knows and nobody cares except those few who know the truth."

"It would be nice to believe we have a handle on the truth—whatever *that* is—but thanks anyway," Gil said. "I owe you, but wouldn't know how to pay you back. You know, Jack, I was probably the most patriotic guy to ever enlist. Maybe I should have gone along to get along like everybody else, but I made my choice and nearly went to jail for it—except for you."

"We were patriots then and we're patriots now. My dad liked to say, 'You pays your penny and takes your choice'. You're the scholar, Gil, why'd we do those things?"

"You first, Jack. What's your take?"

"Oh, some code of male pride in being a soldier on the side of the good guys and doing the right thing—all that stuff I guess."

"Jack, that 'stuff,' as you call it, used to be called 'honor' and 'duty'. Men used to go off to slay a dragon and then come home to be crowned king—or elected sheriff, maybe. But we ran out of dragons, so we had to settle for fighting some crappy little war that nobody liked."

Jack raised his glass. "Whatever it's called, let's hope guys like us never go out of style."

Gil sat in the reception area of Funds-Lot Finance, where Jack was the chief of security. Businesses like Funds-Lot were known in business double-speak as "alternative sources of finance." They lent money at rates that were legal, but just barely. A businessman with poor credit or no credit who needed, for example, $250,000 for thirty days to get his goods out of Customs or to pay a manufacturer might come to Funds-Lot. He would pay an outrageous but legal premium for the use of the money.

Most clients were grateful for this source of money; a few others weren't and tried to skip without paying back the loan. Most were very clever and very resourceful in avoiding repayment. It was Jack's job to avoid bad credit risks and to chase down deadbeats even if they skipped to other countries. He did background checks, he checked for hidden assets, he checked for a Swiss bank account, a red flag. He had contacts with all of the best man-hunters in the world.

Just when the borrower was about to pick up the loan, Jack held what he called a "come-to-Jesus" talk with the borrower. That is when he would explain how most clients who had failed to repay a Funds-Lot loan had either ended up in jail or had been financially crushed by lawsuits. Other deadbeats, not yet run to ground, had arrest warrants pending in a number of jurisdictions. A mere traffic stop could get them arrested.

Jack's secretary showed Gil into Jack's office. The two men shook hands. Jack said, "Sorry to say, pal, last time I saw you was at your wife's funeral. It's been—what—couple of years now? I hope things are better for you now."

"Yes. Thanks, Jack. Now I'm trying to find out who did in my friend."

"The guy at the Buddhist temple? I guessed he was a neighbor of yours. How can I help?"

"You worked a Chinese desk at the CIA."

"I did?"

"Yes, you did, but you didn't tell me; I learned it from the tooth fairy. Now give me a ten-minute course in Chinese espionage."

"Jesus, Gil. I saved your buns once. Now what in hell are you involved in? Screw around in FBI territory and you really will end up in the joint with your pants around your ankles."

"Jack, I'm not dumb enough to play the counterspy. It's just that there's a strong suspicion that David Chang's employers had some hand in his murder."

"And?"

"And I think they're doing some industrial or other kinds of spying, and if they are, then maybe somehow it's connected to David's murder."

"Ten minute's worth, you say? Hope I can I remember that much. Just like us, their MSS has thousands of people operating all over the world to buy or steal military or space technology, patents, equipment—you name it. I don't have figures any more, but they must have hundreds of front businesses in the U.S. alone. It's been awhile for me."

"Jack, give me some idea how they operate here."

"How do they do it? Front businesses are big now, and then there's the usual chicanery—phony journalists, bribes, blackmail—the same way it's been done for hundreds of years. Wouldn't know where to begin. With the Chinese, about ninety-eight percent of these front businesses close without making a profit. So what does that tell you about their real purpose?"

"Anything special about their methods?"

Jack leaned back in his chair. "Hard to generalize, but they never seem to have trouble recruiting Americans of Chinese ancestry. They'll appeal to some sense of obligation to their 'homeland' or maybe they'll suggest that relatives in China might find life a little easier if the person cooperates. Or they might do both."

"Your ancestors came from Ireland; mine from Portugal. Do we feel an obligation to spy for those countries?"

"No, we don't," Jack said, "but then if we weren't two generations removed, maybe we'd be afraid of what they might do to Grandma or Uncle Tim back in the old country. Then there's always money. Money, just money plain and simple drive most spies—not love of the mother country. Others like the feeling of power that comes with making mischief on an international level."

Gil said, "I suppose they're also told that it will help Chinese-American relations and enhance world peace and harmony and tranquility in the long haul."

Jack grabbed a dart from a tray on the credenza behind him and scored a bull's eye on the dartboard behind Gil. "Oh, they do, indeed. They do, indeed, my friend. The controllers have to make such people feel there's something noble and not heinous in the betrayal of the country that gives them a home and a job. Traitors aren't stupid in the intellectual sense, so their handlers have to help them rationalize what they're doing."

"And they want people with credentials, no doubt," Gil said.

"Yes, and they use academic or scientific exchanges, visiting students—just about anything that could be used for cover, they'll use it and have used it. If you care, long-term agents are called 'chen di yu' which means 'fish at the bottom of the ocean'."

"I'll keep that in mind if I find myself on a quiz show."

Jack glared at him, but the glare soon melted into a smile. "Still the wise ass after all these years, aren't you?"

Gil laughed. "I couldn't resist, Jack. So, we'd call him a 'mole' or a 'sleeper'?"

"Same idea. They encourage Chinese who become citizens to apply for sensitive jobs in government, universities, or anywhere they might be able to steal useful information, software, or patents. They may try to activate them years later or never."

"I interviewed a Chinese consulate type who knew these guys David worked for."

"Every country uses diplomatic cover for intelligence people. Some do it more than others do. With the Chinese, I'd assume that every 'diplomat' runs errands for the MSS even if he's not a full-fledged member of that ministry." He paused. "But I'm getting the feeling you know most of this."

"I do and I don't. Sometimes it's useful to have someone confirm something you kind of knew, but never articulated. By the way, Jack, David's daughter is an engineer at Lockard. The papers always mention stealth technology whenever they mention Lockard."

"Hell, if she wouldn't be a good target, I don't know who would be."

"That was one of my first thoughts when this whole thing first started. I think they tried to break the ice with her once or twice, but she blew them off."

"And they let it go that easy? They'll do anything, you know—money, sexual blackmail, but they'll always go for the easy way first."

"What about the high-tech buys?"

"They just go to a seller of equipment on a restricted list and buy it, but then have it shipped to a domestic address. That way the seller doesn't know it's headed to some place like China, Russia, or Iraq. Your guys are working for China, or so it seems."

"And that domestic address," Gil said, "is a freight forwarder who doctors the shipping documents to hide the true destination?"

"You got it," Jack said. "The item may be re-shipped to a country friendly to the U.S. where another freight-forwarder ships it to China."

Both men sat silent for a few moments. Finally, Gil said, "Jack, I just don't know. I want to nail these guys if they killed David, but I think I'm out of my depth and now I'm wondering if I haven't bitten too much off."

"Gil, it's never any fun just treading along on the surface of life. Makes it dull and no fun. We all need a good barroom brawl now and then to make us feel alive."

"Wouldn't know, Jack. Sounds like your Irish talking, but I don't qualify as a brawler of your caliber. I'm too much of a pussy."

"Yeah, right. I know what you can do to a guy who thinks you're a pussy. Go get the bastards. Maybe you can have some fun, too."

"Fun? You kidding me, Jack?"

"No. Even if you can't find your friend's killer, maybe you can screw up their little mission for the MSS."

"Didn't you just tell me not to get myself involved in FBI territory?"

"So I lied." Jack grinned. "I'm getting a charge just talking about this. If you need any help, give me a holler."

"I can use your help. If you can do one thing without getting yourself in trouble ... ?"

"What's that, Gil?"

"See if any of your contacts still working at The Company have any info on this character Zhiyuan—Jeff—Ming. He's evidently a graduate of the Beijing College of International Relations. I don't know how common his names might be, but I'm counting on your contacts having a dossier on a guy of apparent importance."

"His training alone could make him someone who would kill you or me quick as you can spit, but I'll make a few phone calls. Best I can do," Jack said.

"I couldn't ask for more. Let me get out of your face—unless you'll let me buy you lunch."

"Not today, Gil. Too much to do, but thanks just the same."

The two men stood and shook hands, gripping each other's shoulder as they did so.

It was just past midday. Having had only a cup of coffee for breakfast, Gil was hungry. More than that, he needed a few moments to mull over his talk with Jack. He stopped at a family-owned burger joint on Valley Boulevard. He hadn't had a thick, greasy burger and onion rings in awhile and so felt entitled to them. He convinced himself that he would eat little or nothing for dinner to offset the fat he would now consume. He sat at a table by a window that faced a parking lot, where a group of Latina high school girls were setting up a car wash, using the owner's hose faucet. Their hand-lettered sign said they were raising money for their theater club and its production of "West Side Story." They wore their standard uniform—white shorts, tank tops and running shoes. Gil wondered who would play Maria.

Gil wolfed his burger, covered with a thick tomato slice, thousand-island sauce, and lettuce. He nibbled at his remaining onion rings, made from real onion slices. His talk with Jack had him both energized and afraid all at the same time. Again, he could only hope that he hadn't stepped in it. He and his lady were both suspects in a murder he had pledged to help solve. But, if he got too close to David's killer, then he, too, might end up dead. Gil now had a lot to mull over, not the least of which was Hara's offhand expression of hope that Gil hadn't been set up in some way.

He tried to dodge the kids' car wash by leaving through the opposite door, but a girl ambushed him. She seemed about sixteen, but used a baby-talk voice to ask, "Sir, would you like a car wash? It's free, but you can make a donation for our theater club, if you like."

"No school today, young lady?"

"Half day—teachers' conference," she said.

Gil dangled his car key. "You have a driver's license?"

"Concepcion does." She pointed to a girl who seemed to be the leader.

"Tell Concepcion to be careful and don't take all day." He shouted after her. "Oh, and those papers on the floor—throw them out."

Gil returned to the counter for a cup of coffee that was strong enough to clean an engine block. His car did need a wash; it always needed a wash, but he welcomed the interruption and the chance to linger over some coffee and to mull over Jack's comments a bit longer.

In about twenty minutes, Concepcion squealed the tires of his car when she re-parked it so Gil would know it was ready. He thanked her, told her to break a leg with their stage production, gave her a handful of singles and drove off. The coffee had offset the effects of the heavy lunch, and Gil felt more alert now.

It was time to think out his next move. If Jack's suppositions about Ming were correct, Gil knew he could be dealing with a dangerous man.

CHAPTER NINETEEN

Gil stopped by his office to check his mail and messages. He was expecting a check, but it hadn't yet arrived in the mail, and some of Gil's creditors would have to wait another day or two. The receptionist in the common area put her caller on hold so she could stop Gil. "Did your friend find you, Mr. Rodrigues?"

"I'm sorry, Rose, what friend?"

"Mr. Nguyen stopped by. He said he hadn't seen you in years and hoped to surprise you. He asked what kind of work you did. I gave him one of your cards."

"Did he leave a phone number, Rose?"

"He said he left his cards in the car and would go and get one, but he never came back."

"What did he look like, Rose?"

"His name's Vietnamese, but he looked ethnic Chinese. It was hard to tell. He was a younger man and kind of athletic looking. He asked me if you drove a Jaguar. I'm sorry I laughed when he asked that." She giggled. "I told him you drove an old Nissan. I hope you don't mind my telling him—I mean about your old car."

"That's okay, Rose. Thanks."

Gil had no current acquaintances named Nguyen. Gil knew that half of the population of Vietnam had the name of Nguyen.

Gil's office was locked as he had left it; nothing seemed disturbed. Who this character could be he could only guess. Gil had two messages. One was from Hara, the other from Ming. Gil couldn't imagine what Ming wanted, but he returned Hara's call first. Hara's tone was that of someone announcing the winner of the office football pool and Gil found it annoying.

"Gil, I spoke with the DA. We're going to pass on your offer to take a polygraph. You do know, don't you, that you and Diana always were low on our list of suspects?"

"Steve, I hope you don't expect me to thank you for sparing me more sleepless nights, because that's not going to happen. Until you told me that Diana and I were suspects, I regarded you as the homicide expert, but you've blown this one so far. I plan to continue digging on David's murder. Just try to stop me."

"Gil ... " He cut Hara off by hanging up on him.

Immediately he felt ashamed of his unforgiving conduct toward Hara's attempt at conciliation, but he would let it lie for now. He knew Hara was man enough to know he had been a jerk in suspecting him and Diana. They could make up over some sweet and sour shrimp or a beer on another day when he felt more charitable. Besides, Gil liked Hara and wanted to remain friends with him.

Gil expected that Quon must have phoned Ming after his meeting with Gil at the Chinese Consulate, and that call had to have generated today's message from Ming. On the return call, Ming was at his personable best. "Mr. Rodrigues, have you ever eaten at the Mandarin Red Dragon?"

"Yes. Great Cantonese and Sichuan dishes. Great seafood." Gil meant it; it was a fine restaurant and one of seven owned by the same family. Contrary to conventional wisdom, some of the best Chinese restaurants were part of small family-owned chains and it was common to see as few as only one or two non-Asians in such places. Their downside was their large, open and typically noisy eating areas. The well-heeled reserved private dining rooms.

"Good," Ming said. "Would 8 P.M. be convenient? I wish to discuss some business with you."

There was no plastic décor in the lobby of the Mandarin Red Dragon. Instead, its lobby was filled with hand-carved cherry wood dragons, enameled panels, dynasty vases, and, of course, a laughing Buddha facing the door.

The maitre d' was expecting Gil. "Mr. Rodrigues, I presume? Mr. Hoa will show you to Mr. Ming's table." He had a British accent and Gil guessed that he was from Hong Kong.

Ming was waiting in one of several private dining rooms, each of which had one or more waiters assigned exclusively to it. Gil tried to remember a time when he would have been impressed, but he was hungry and eager to find out what Ming was up to.

Ming stood as Gil entered and beckoned for Gil to sit facing the door.

"To what do I owe the honor?"

"So you're familiar with the Chinese custom, Mr. Rodrigues?"

"I read a lot."

"You do, indeed. Yes, among my people, the chairs facing the door are for honored guests. How much more of our culture you know I can only guess."

The waiter took orders for their drinks. As in many Chinese restaurants, the more conventional mixed drinks were unavailable. Gil ordered a dry martini. "Make that two," Ming said. "I've taken the liberty of ordering appetizers," Ming continued, "I take it you prefer genuine Chinese food over the atrocities that pass for it in your country?"

Gil suspected that even the small talk was a set-up for something, but he went along. " It's a fair question that I've been asked more than once. I think I know genuine. Chinese restaurants have been here in America for about one hundred and twenty-five years and the best of them are in California and Chicago."

"But that was after we built your railroads."

"Is that where we're headed—the exploitation of Chinese peasants by the evil American railroad barons? Everyone built railroads here—Chinese, Irish, Germans, Italians, Blacks, Indians—they all did their share of brute labor."

"You know your history, too."

"As I said, I read a lot."

The drinks arrived. Ming lifted his glass to touch Gil's. It made an audible click. "When we toast in China, we say *'gan bei'*. It means 'empty glass', but you knew that, too, didn't you?"

The appetizers arrived and Gil had to wonder if Ming did anything without a secondary motive. The waiter set out paper-wrapped chicken, and pork spare ribs. He also set out "drunk shrimp"—live crayfish wiggling and soaking in white wine. One pulled them apart with one's fingers, stripping away the hard covering and eating the meat.

Ming's eyes widened reflexively and Gil knew he expected him to show some kind of squeamishness. Gil kept a poker face, then grabbed a wriggling crayfish and ate it in the prescribed manner. He then sipped his drink and grinned at Ming in the knowledge he had spoiled his fun.

"You said you wanted to talk business." Gil twirled the stem of his martini glass.

Ming paused, then looked at Gil. "My charter here in your country is fairly broad. To help China's economy move forward under market economy socialism as defined by our leaders, businesses such as my primary employer have been chartered with identifying products and technologies in both the U.S. and Europe that will help to further that progress." He added, "I may have alluded to this when you stopped by our offices."

"A cynic might say your mission statement came from a company brochure."

"Yes, you caught me. Those are words I've borrowed, I must confess." Ming smiled sheepishly at having been discovered.

"And that same cynic might say that means you steal anything you can, to be copied or counterfeited in China—preferably without paying license or royalty fees."

Ming strained to be affable. "Steal? You do me wrong, Mr. Rodrigues. Now it is you who spouts propaganda. Next you will speak of 'the Yellow Peril'."

"No, that's last century's war cry. Gotta keep it current." Gil became conciliatory. He didn't want to discourage Ming from making his play. "But it does sound like a challenge, as we used to say in corporate America, after having been saddled with some dumb-ass project. What does it mean in plain English?"

"It means I could use the help of an astute American in identifying products and acquiring them. With your business and investigative background, I believe you—how do you say?—'fit the bill'."

"DaleeAhn—your company—a client of mine? Is that what you have in mind? Why do I ask? Because I'll never be an employee of anyone again."

"Why yes, we'd be your client and I'd pay your standard fees, to which we might add a premium of sorts."

"I charge by the hour plus mileage and expenses."

"Would a retainer—that is the word, is it not—of, say, twenty thousand dollars be adequate, Mr. Rodrigues?"

"It would be more than adequate, considering that my corporate clients seldom go with retainers."

"Then it's agreed, Mr. Rodrigues?"

"I never lead people on, Mr. Ming, but I couldn't make that decision on the spur of the moment. I'd have to think about it."

"A reasonable request. When might I have your decision? The retainer is available in cash, if you so desire to be paid that way."

"I'll let you know."

Ming offered another toast. "*Gan bei.*" They again touched glasses. Gil had been at Chinese dinners where the toasts, offered almost by the minute, resulted in everyone in attendance becoming hopelessly sloshed. Such frequency wasn't his custom, but he went along with it that night.

Ming asked, "On a different subject, do you enjoy the tables in Las Vegas?"

"Somehow I don't think you'd have asked me if you didn't already know the answer."

"I mention it only because my colleague and I plan to go there this weekend. I could book a flight and a room for you. You could gamble on my tab and maybe we could avail ourselves of some female companionship. Or you could bring your own if you're not interested in some variety."

"Too much action can wear a man out. On the other hand, would you be talking about one of those showgirls whose legs go on forever?"

Ming leered. "I'm sure it can be arranged if that's your taste."

Gil forced an expression of disappointment. "I'd enjoy both, but I'm going to pass."

"Pity you can't help us enjoy Las Vegas."

"To be sure," Gil said, "there's certainly enough guilty pleasures to be had there. It's fun to bring one's lady along and get one's table fix several times a year."

"Then you won't be surprised to hear that I enjoy Asian Stud and Pai Gow, both variations on your American poker games."

"I stick with Blackjack." Gil said, "Craps and poker require more thought than I care to invest in a casino game."

Ming smiled. "I find it hard to believe that you avoid thought in any endeavor, but I think I know what you mean."

"Changing the subject for a moment, has anyone spoken to you about David's murder?"

"Why, yes. A sheriff's deputy of Chinese ancestry interviewed my partner and me."

"Were you able to help his investigation in any way?"

"Somehow I doubt if we did. He asked us questions one might

expect: Did we know of any problems David might have had with money, gambling, women and so forth."

"And you knew of none, I can guess. Did he ask about your whereabouts on the night of the murder?"

"As I said, Mr. Rodrigues, he asked the expected questions. My partner and I were at the apartment we share. We were watching a program on the Asian Cable Channel—a costume drama called 'Palace Betrayal'. It takes place in the sixteenth century. Awful, too, I might add."

"Can anyone confirm that?"

Ming smiled. "That the costume drama was awful or that we were in our apartment?" He shook his head. "I'm sorry. That was a feeble joke. But you do sound just like the investigating detective. He asked the same question and the answer is that it would be difficult to confirm because we didn't talk to anyone in our apartment complex that evening."

"I guess it's my line of work that makes me think like a cop even though I'm not one of them. Did you make any phone calls?"

Ming flashed another one of his smiles, only this one had a forced quality to it. "That you're not one of them is their loss it would seem. And, Detective Chin also asked about the calls. No, we made no calls from the apartment that evening."

" Did any other tenants see you that evening?"

"I'm afraid not, Mr. Rodrigues."

Ming sipped his drink and added, "By the way, I have tentative plans to return to China next week. I'm not sure how long I'll be there at this moment. I have a multiple-entry visa to your country and it expires in two months."

"I've had to make my share of trips to the home office when I was in business, too. It's always a cause for anxiety. You never know when you might be walking into an ambush for not doing the job right." Gil forced a grin. He was certain he detected a hint of fear in Ming's eyes.

"Are you sure you can't accept our offer of employment, Mr. Rodrigues? Do you find the pay inadequate or the work not to your liking?"

"I've too many other commitments now," Gil said. "Best we leave it that way, but it's nice you think my talents are worth that kind of money."

Ming signaled for the check. Gil thanked him for the dinner and accepted his handshake and goodbyes.

Gil called Sabrina at her desk the next day. "Ming offered me a job last night and a good time in Vegas."

"Uncle, I won't even ask if you accepted. I know the answer. What's he up to, that creep?"

"That should be obvious, honey. He knows that you, your mom, I and maybe—just maybe—Hara all think he had something to do with your dad's murder."

"But thinking doesn't make it so, Unc."

"That's right, and although I think we have a motive, we need to place him, or someone he hired, at the scene for a conviction. In his homeland they would just beat it out of him. They wouldn't bother with such niceties as circumstantial or physical evidence."

Sabrina sighed audibly. "It's awful how they treat people. And, true to form, he wants to buy you off. Everyone's for sale in his view of the world, so why not you, too?"

"Well, it doesn't take the IRS to figure out that a guy like me who drives a five-year-old Nissan isn't exactly rolling in the bucks and just might fade into the sunset for the right amount of chump change."

"I know you wouldn't, Uncle Gil. You'd never sell out."

"Don't be too idealistic. My Irish father-in-law used to warn against confusing a shiny penny with the sun. To you, I'm that shiny penny. Don't mistake me for the sun. Sometimes I think everyone really does have a price. I just haven't figured out mine yet."

"You'd let that snake buy you off?"

"I told him I had to think about it. Helen and I always did like the blackjack tables. He'd take you, too, if I suggested it."

"You're teasing. I'll believe it when I see it. Did you ask him if he knew anything?"

"Yes I'm teasing and yes I asked him, but frankly I didn't expect him to say anything he hasn't already told the sheriff's office. He's much too cool. Right now I've got to worry about something else."

"Which is?"

"He's talking about heading back to China—maybe next week. If he killed your dad, he just might get away."

"That would be awful, Unc.

"Awful indeed, honey, and a crime in itself. I've got to get moving."

The message light on Gil's answer machine was blinking when he arrived at his office. "Gil. It's Jack. Call me."

Such a quick callback could only mean one thing: Jack had learned something. The message was only a few minutes old, so he was able to reach Jack at his desk.

"You have something, Jack?" Gil couldn't conceal his excitement.

"I called a former colleague. He and I worked overlapping areas. He liked to interview Chinese dissidents who managed to get out of China."

"If they were dissidents, Jack, how did they get out?"

"That's all part of what I have for you. If they feel these dissidents have been sufficiently 'reeducated'—brainwashed—or just plain scared silly by the fear of what might happen to family left behind—then sometimes they let them out."

"I think I know where this is headed, Jack."

"My friend recalls several of these dissidents in particular. We've heard it all before so many times. People sent to labor camps where they were forced to stand facing a wall for nine, ten days and shocked with electric prods. After that, they were sent to brainwashing, or 'reeducation', as they call it there."

"From Stalin to Mao, change the names, but the game's the same," Gil said.

"The people in charge of this reeducation just assume that if they don't kick the crap out of these people, they'll remain a threat to the government."

"Stalin just shot them."

"The Chinese shoot a few, too, but it's more effective to torture them and then put them back into the general population as examples."

"I'm waiting for the punch line, Jack."

"These dissidents my friend interviewed said that one of the government interrogators seemed to especially enjoy his work. That man has the same Chinese name as your Jeff Ming."

"Could it be just a case of having the same names, Jack?"

"That's always possible, of course, but unlikely in this case, given his training at that school run by the MSS, as you've learned—what you've told me plus the general circumstances."

Gil thanked Jack for the information, but there was a part of him that wished the story on Ming was that he had been just some harmless, middle-aged guy who taught English to high school kids somewhere in China. Now Gil needed to move fast. He had constructed a scenario of David's murder, but had little faith in it until now. To test his scenario, he had to cover ground already covered by Hara and Chin. They had to have missed something—or someone.

CHAPTER TWENTY

Gil drove to the parking lot of the Buddhist temple where David had last been seen alive. David had been seen in the lot, but not in the temple conference room, where he would normally meet with his study group. From the parking lot Gil drove to the house in front of which David's body had been found in his car. The distance was less than two blocks. The houses were mostly two-story and about twenty years old. Little on the surface distinguished the street from any number of others in Southern California except for its proximity to the temple—a fact that bumped up the market value of the houses. The vegetation was typical Southern California tract home—oleander, mountain laurel, yucca trees, bird of paradise and some date and royal palms. A number of older eucalyptus trees blocked the sun in the day and street lamps at night. The sheer number of cars in driveways and on the street suggested a mature neighborhood of two and three-car families with driving teenagers and commuting parents.

Garden hose in hand, a man in his seventies wearing shorts and Michigan State tee shirt watered the lawn at the house in front of which David's body had been found. The lawn had a watering system, but watering by hand must have given the man something to do, not to mention the opportunity to watch his neighbors' comings and goings. Gil gave him half a wave and a smile as if he knew him, then made a "K" turn and parked in front of the man's house. He walked up the driveway to avoid the wet grass and stopped about five feet from the man.

"You from the *Trib*?" the man asked, before Gil spoke.

"No sir." Older people always responded better to a measure of formal courtesy. "I was a friend and neighbor of the murdered man," Gil offered. "Our kids went to school together. My name is Gil Rodrigues. I'm a private investigator. I live here in town. And you, sir, are … ?"

"Craig English," the man answered, and extended his hand after wiping the moisture from the hose onto his tee shirt. "I'm sorry about your friend, Mister … ?"

"Chang," Gil offered. "David Chang."

English turned off the hose at the faucet. "What do you expect to find here that the sheriff hasn't?"

"Something that might tell us who did it, Mr. English. I can't help the dead, but maybe I can do something for the living."

"A Lieutenant Hara and a Chinese detective came by. I had to tell them I didn't see or hear anything until the next morning when I spotted the body and dialed 911. No idea when it happened."

"They think it happened around 8 P.M. Hard to believe no one was coming or going at that time, with all the cars around here."

"Like I told the lieutenant, Mr. Rodrigues, this is a quiet neighborhood. Some Halloween pranks, teenagers peeling rubber with their dad's car—that sort of thing—but nothing like this has ever happened here. I've got to believe anyone who saw anything would have said something by now."

Gil knew that if he was to avoid covering ground already covered by Hara he had to think outside the box. "You're retired, Mr. English?"

"Last five years. I taught at Citrus Grove Junior High."

"You see people coming and going. Think for a moment, sir—who besides yourself *could* have seen something?"

"I mentioned the Johnson girl to the lieutenant. She lives next door, but she mustn't have seen anything because I saw them go to her door, and they were gone a few minutes later."

"Why her, Mr. English, over others in the neighborhood?"

English's tone became conspiratorial and leering. "She sneaks out of the house to make out with her boyfriend in his car. They park three, four doors down under that eucalyptus tree. Her dad is a Bible thumper and real strict. He probably thinks she's in her room, but my wife and I see her sneaking out. We call 'em 'Romeo and Juliet'. The dad would blow a gasket if he knew."

Gil smiled so as not to let the gossip appear unappreciated. "And the night of the murder?"

"I'm not sure. My wife and I ran some errands and were running in and out, what with food shopping and some other trips, getting ready for a barbecue on the weekend. I think I saw the boyfriend's car, but didn't see her with him, but not seeing her head doesn't mean she wasn't in the car—if you get my drift." This time English delivered an exaggerated wink in case Gil had missed something.

"About what time?"

"Oh, between seven and eight. Dan Rather was just finishing up around 7:30 or thereabouts."

"Anyone else, Mr. English?"

"That's about it, but I figure if the boyfriend was around, then the Johnson kid must have been diddlin' around with him at some time or other that night. You plan to talk to her?"

"Yes, I'd hope to."

"Be sure to talk with the dad first, Mr. Rodrigues."

"You're saying he's dangerous?"

"No. It's just that he's an Old Testament type. Rules his home the same way. Don't know how his wife puts up with it."

"Thanks for the heads-up, Mr. English." They shook hands. The man went back to his watering and waved to Gil as he pulled away.

Gil stopped for some Thai take-out and took it back to his office where he just picked at it. He thought he remembered having left a beer in his little office fridge, but he was wrong and had to settle for some tea he made with one of those little immersible travel gadgets that heated a single cup of water. He made a note on his desk pad to pick up teabags and beer. He added the words, "clean refrigerator."

Gil's limitations gnawed at him. He wasn't a homicide investigator, but he knew that an organization like the FBI would interview every member of every household on the street where the murder took place. They would talk with the monks and nuns at the temple and with David's family, friends, and employer. They would talk to Gil. They'd get it done no matter how many trips it took. Hara knew this, too, but his resources were limited as well. He and his men would talk to those living only within two or three doors of the murder scene, leave their calling cards, and rely on tipsters or witnesses to come forward. Only high-profile murders got the full treatment.

Unspoken was the understanding that the murder of an obscure accountant didn't qualify for star treatment. Buddhists weren't likely to picket the sheriff's station to demand results, but some politically ambitious Asians just might. And Gil knew, too, that he couldn't talk to everyone either; he had a living to make, his commitment to Sabrina and David's widow notwithstanding. He had to hope that his rifle approach would pay off faster than a shotgun, approach.

It was approaching six, his usual cocktail hour, but that would have to wait. Gil always took care of business first. He started to put the uneaten portion of his shrimp and rice into his tiny refrigerator, but changed his mind and decided to trash it in the outside dumpster so his office wouldn't smell of garlic and ginger the next day. He checked his dress and ran a comb through his hair in the men's room before leaving for the Johnsons' house a little past

6:00 P.M. He expected Mr. English to observe his return to the street. English didn't disappoint him and even waved when he saw Gil emerge from his car.

Gil found the Johnson's at home. A teenage girl answered the door. This had to be his Juliet. Her hairstyle and eyeglasses had a retro, vaguely fifties look; otherwise she was blond, blue-eyed and high school pretty. It struck Gil that with the area's radical population shift from white to Asian and Hispanic, girls like her must have become anomalies among her schoolmates. "Hi, I'm Gil Rodrigues. Are your parents in?"

The girl turned and, without opening the screen door, shouted, "Dad!"

A man in his forties looked out at Gil. He, too, did not open the screen door. His eyes were expressionless. He wore a Dutch-style beard Gil had rarely seen outside of Pennsylvania. In the living room beyond the small foyer, Gil could see a portrait of Jesus on the wall along with a crucifix and some samplers, the wording of which was not discernible from where Gil stood. The girl stood about four feet behind Mr. Johnson with eyes widened in a way that suggested more apprehension than curiosity.

The man was clearly hostile so Gil adopted voice and body language intended to be as disarming as possible. He took two small steps back, dropped his hands to his sides and looked at the man's chest. Eye contact could be a threat. Gil had learned long ago that it's not productive to look hostile people in the eye, or to patronize them either.

"What can I do for you?" The man's tone implied that Gil's question was a challenge and not a request for information.

Gil smiled. "Good evening. Mr. Johnson, I presume?"

"Yes, that's me." His face remained expressionless.

"I'm Gil Rodrigues. I'm here about the murder that was committed out in front here several days ago. The sheriff's people believe my friend Mr. Chang was murdered some time in the early evening. In other words, they don't think the body was dumped here. I was hoping to find someone here on the street who might have seen someone or something that night."

"We told the sheriff we didn't see anything. Why would you think anything's changed?"

Gil tried to be conciliatory. "Adults—teenagers—they come and go, what with shopping, school affairs, dates. Sometimes we remember something that didn't occur to us first time we were asked."

"My daughter's in the house during the school week and we didn't see anything, Mr. Rodrigues. We can't help you. Goodnight."

Johnson started to turn away. Gil held out a business card. "Mr. Johnson—please—take my card just in case." Johnson stared at Gil who repeated in a voice just above a whisper, "Please."

Johnson opened the screen door, took the card and turned away without saying anything further. That gave Gil the opportunity to make eye contact with the girl for several seconds, after which she turned abruptly on her heel and walked out of the foyer.

He played and replayed the tape of his eye contact with the Johnson girl. Did she suspect that Gil knew something her dad didn't? He had to hope so. Would she talk if she felt safe? He would wait before trying further contact with her, but he hadn't yet figured what form that contact should take. Gil never counted on luck and he didn't want to tick off Hara, but his intuition was holding and he had to hope that his star-crossed Juliet might help him nail it when it was all said and done.

His message light was blinking when he arrived at his office the next day. He listened to the message twice even though he got it first time. He hoped it meant what he wanted it to mean. The message and the visit to the Johnson house had to be connected, barring coincidence—and Gil wouldn't bet on coincidence. The message on Gil's voice mail was from a Jane Macy, a name Gil thought he had heard before, but didn't know where. She said only that she was a counselor at La Subida High School and that she needed to speak with Gil. When he returned her call she said only that it would be best if he stopped by the school during school hours because she didn't want to get into the matter on the phone. They set an appointment for the next day.

CHAPTER TWENTY-ONE

Gil continued to trust his feelings on this one. He had to. He didn't have a staff to sit around and do analyses and run down slender leads. He had learned that intuition wasn't supernatural. It was as real and as natural as heartbeat and breath. He saw it as the unconscious assessment of facts, cues and observations that could lead us to a conclusion or at least to an accurate guess. The human brain worked in ways not yet mapped out.

Gil's intuition regarding that day's trip to a local high school told him that it would be worthwhile. Hara hadn't said another word about him and Diana being suspects. Gil attributed it to Hara's own good sense, and he had no plans to reopen that can of worms.

Gil's kids had graduated from La Subida High School, but Gil hadn't set foot on the campus since they had graduated ten and twelve years ago respectively. He arrived at the tail end of a lunch period. He crossed the campus on his way to the administrative offices. Asians, Hispanics and white kids clustered on benches, under trees and breezeways and on the low walls of flower beds which contained more candy wrappers than plants. The doors and woodwork needed painting. The students were self-segregated by race and sex. The nerds carried backpacks; those too cool for school carried nothing.

A receptionist whose buttocks were at least two sizes larger than her clerical chair was designed for directed Gil to a row of offices. She offered Gil a cookie from a tray lined with a white paper doily.

"They're homemade with lots of real butter," she announced.

Gil politely refused, patting his abdomen as he did so. "Thanks. Gotta watch my girlish figure," he said with a grin.

Outside of the offices and along an opposite wall were benches with students holding "referral" slips. They were all boys, most of whom returned Gil's casual glance with a surly glare. He guessed most were there for disrupting class, or other school crimes and misdemeanors, and they would receive whatever passed for discipline, which the counselors would mete out.

Jane Macy's office door was closed. When Gil knocked, Macy opened the door just enough for Gil to identify himself, after which she ushered him in and offered him an empty chair. Seated in the chairs that on either side of him were the Johnson girl and a boy who appeared to be about her age.

"We've never met, Mr. Rodrigues, but I knew your late wife when we both taught in elementary. She was very sweet and we all miss her. Someone here knew her, too."

"That's kind of you," Gil said. "Thank you."

Macy glanced at the two teenagers as if to check whether they had absorbed the exchange, then looked at Gil. "Apparently you've met LeeAnne Johnson, but I don't think you know Mike Hernandez."

Gil offered his hand to Hernandez, who had not yet learned that a conventional handshake between adult males included a measure of firmness in the grip. "Nice meeting you, Mike." He turned to the girl. "LeeAnne, I have a feeling this meeting was your idea."

"It was theirs and mine," Macy said, tapping a business card—which could only be the one that Gil left at the Johnson house—on the knuckle of her opposite thumb.

"LeeAnne and Mike tell me they saw something that night—the night of the murder."

Gil found himself searching for a response that would mask his excitement. "That's wonderful," he managed. "Have you talked to Lieutenant Hara from the sheriff's office?"

"He's my next call, Mr. Rodrigues, but how Mike and LeeAnne saw what they saw is a bit of—well, let's just say—a 'sensitive boy-girl matter'."

"Understood. Your dad didn't know you were out front with Mike. All of us old fogies were young once—hard as that is to believe at your age." Gil looked to Macy for agreement. Macy's eyes widened and she smiled without saying anything.

"Has your dad ever hit you, LeeAnne?" Gil wanted the question to catch the girl off guard. It did. She didn't answer, but looked at the floor.

Macy cut him off. "I'll deal with those issues, if you don't mind, Mr. Rodrigues. Mike, LeeAnne—tell this man what you told me."

Gil slid his chair back to allow better eye contact between his Romeo and Juliet. They both spoke at the same time. "We … "

They chuckled, after which the girl deferred to the boy. "We were sitting in my car—just talking," Mike began. "I park about four doors down from LeeAnne—uh, her dad doesn't like her hanging out with me—at least not during the week. Then LeeAnne said, 'somebody's coming'."

Gil turned to LeeAnne. "You saw? You heard?"

"I heard footsteps, but didn't know from where at first, but then it was kind of weird."

"Weird, you say?"

The books on interviewing say that one shouldn't interrupt an eyewitness who's talking. Gil knew that, but had to bite his tongue to conceal his excitement and to keep from pressing the girl for amplification.

"Yeah, weird. He wasn't on the sidewalk. He was walking down the middle of the street real fast—not running, but walking real fast."

Gil had to ask, "Do you think he saw you?"

"No." The child woman blushed. "Mike and I sort of squished down in the seat and we heard him walk by."

"You were facing towards Mr. English's house and he was coming from that direction? Did you see where he went?"

The boy spoke. "We heard a car door close a few doors behind us and then we heard the car drive away. We figured it was them because they were gone when we looked up."

"Now it's 'them', you say?"

Mike continued. "Yeah. The man got into the passenger side and the car did a U-turn and they drove away."

"Could you identify either one?"

Hernandez looked at his girlfriend who shrugged her shoulders. "It was dark. The guy in the street looked Asian. Maybe he was Chinese." The boy grinned. "But you know what they say about my own people?"

Macy spoke. "What's that Mike?"

He laughed at his answer. "We all look alike."

Gil was solemn. "This is very important. You're saying then that he was definitely Asian, but you couldn't pick him out in a crowd?"

The young man looked at the young woman and both shook their heads.

Gil looked at the girl and then the boy. "Was he carrying anything?"

The question evoked an almost simultaneous response. The girl spoke first. "The guy in the street was carrying a briefcase and his hand was real white looking."

"White looking? Could he have been wearing some kind of glove?"

"Yeah, I guess it could be a glove. I only got a quick look before we slid down on the seat."

"So you both ducked when you saw him coming. Then you came up for air to see his backside as he walked towards a car?"

They nodded.

"So when he was closest to you before you ducked, you couldn't see his face enough to identity him if you saw him today? What about the car? Could you identify it?"

Mike spoke. "It looked like a German job—maybe a Mercedes or BMW. Like I said, the car did a U-turn and headed out."

"And clothing? You recall what he was wearing?"

"A golf jacket," the girl said excitedly. "And he had his left hand in his pocket."

Gil and Jane Macy looked at each other without speaking for several seconds. Gil had to believe that Macy was thinking the same thing: No murder weapon had been found, so the killer had either walked away with it in his hand or under his clothing. That meant that it was likely, if not certain, that he would have killed the two kids if he had known that they were in that car and could place him at the scene of the crime. Whether Gil's teen lovers had figured that out yet, Gil didn't know, but he wasn't going to be the one to tell them.

Life is full of close calls, he thought. Some are obvious; others unrecognized until long after the event, if ever.

"You kids are doing the right thing you know. Anything else I should know?"

LeeAnne dusted some lint off of her skirt and looked at Macy. "My dad will be mad."

Gil's tone was irritated. "Miss Johnson—LeeAnne—you need to discuss that with Mrs. Macy and the sheriff, if need be. You do understand that, don't you?"

The girl nodded yes. Her eyes widened. She then flashed a big smile and added, "Mrs. Rodrigues was my teacher in the fifth grade. I kind of like figured you were her husband, but I wasn't sure until Mrs. Macy said so. She was real nice, your wife."

Gil looked at the girl for a moment and smiled. "I'm touched by your affection for her. I guess what goes 'round comes 'round after all."

LeeAnne smiled at Gil and Jane Macy, and then averted her eyes as the two adults looked benignly at her.

Gil thanked the three and made his good-byes.

In his car, Gil made notes of his conversation on a clipboard he always carried in his car. "Write it down" was one of the first rules of investigation, but scribbling during an interview inhibited some people, so Gil had learned to avoid it whenever possible.

Lieutenant Hara was irritated that the two teenagers had talked to Gil first. It showed in his voice when Gil called him later in the day. "Steve, don't get your hackles up. It was just a matter of timing that those two kids spoke with me first. They told Macy their story and she had called both of us when the girl insisted she wanted to talk with me first."

That seemed to mollify Hara even if he didn't believe it.

Gil asked, "Steve, is it safe to say that the only prints on or in David's car were his or family members'?"

"You guessed right, Gil. That's why what these kids saw is interesting, but with no positive ID, we still can't place any viable suspects at the scene or in the car."

"And Ming and the other bozo have unshakable alibis, no doubt."

"Well, they've got an alibi we can't prove or disprove, unless you've got some bright ideas."

"Steve, I'd never second-guess you." It didn't bother Gil to pacify Hara because he respected people who did dangerous police work and he had reached an age that made it hard to carry grudges.

"So," Gil thought, "the two kids told Hara what they told me about an Asian man walking from the direction of the house where

David was found." The "white-looking" hand could mean only one thing: latex or cotton gloves to prevent fingerprints. And that could only mean a well-planned murder. Gil knew that Hara had to have come to the same conclusion, and he knew Hara would feel thoroughly frustrated by the inability of the young witnesses to provide positive ID.

Ming and his colleague both drove German cars. Even without a positive identification by the two kids, those new facts alone confirmed Ming and his associate as Gil's prime suspects. To help Hara and the DA get a conviction, however, he would need to tie them to the scene or the crime itself with something solid—something to nail it down for the prosecution and a jury.

That could prove difficult. It was beginning to look impossible. By now, Gil had to assume that Ming knew how to pull off an assassination without leaving the kind of evidence needed in the U.S. for a conviction. And he likely had training, if not practice, doing it in another life working for China's MSS.

However, Gil was still making progress in other areas. He had seen the company books and he knew about the illegal exports. And, he had gotten the teen lovers to tell what they saw. That Gil had been two steps ahead of the official investigation from the beginning might not sit well with Hara's ego, but it meant that Gil was doing his best to keep his promise to Sabrina.

Beyond question, Ming had been lining his pockets through embezzlement. David had to have known about that theft, of course, and gone along with it, but he hadn't been rewarded for his acquiescence either. Quon, who shared a special bond with Ming, had likely been sharing in the take, too, and so would never have blown the whistle on Ming.

David's uncle, however, had been one of Ming's bosses, and Gil could only surmise that Ming had found that reality intolerable.

CHAPTER TWENTY-TWO

Gil had never been tailed—at least in any way he had been aware of. But the car behind was just too close for just too long and had made just too many identical turns and lane changes. Even though tailing wasn't Gil's strong point, he guessed the man was an amateur. Someone experienced in tailing wouldn't have been so obvious. And if lawmen were tailing him, they would probably use several cars that switched position to the front and rear and Gil wouldn't likely notice unless they screwed up in some way.

Or, they could hide a homing device in his car and would know his whereabouts down to the square yard. Furthermore, the law had no reason to tail him; tailing was an expensive operation that ate up time—time best reserved for serious crimes and criminal suspects—not for some obscure PI and solid citizen who scratched out a living doing insurance fraud cases.

The man was so close that even through the refractive distortion of the rear view mirror, Gil could see that the man was young and Asian. He was so close Gil could see his smile. Then it struck him and he felt stupid. He had been missing the obvious: The man *wanted* Gil to know he was being followed. He wrote down the license plate number on the clipboard always beside him on the passenger seat. Reading its mirror image meant reading each letter and number slowly and carefully, but he got it all. The car was an Acura with a V6 that gave the driver the additional acceleration needed to stay so close to Gil.

At this point, Gil was more puzzled than afraid because he felt relatively safe in a car. He could pull into a busy parking lot at a mini mall, post office, police or fire station. There, someone out to do him serious harm would have to think twice because there were bound to be witnesses or even video cameras outside to tape who comes and goes. And, the man tailing him might assume Gil had a cell phone that would allow him to call the law and lead the man into a confrontation with police.

Gil would gamble that his tail, whoever he was, wanted to warn, frighten, or otherwise intimidate him in some way or other. Anyone with legitimate motives would have phoned or made an appointment with him. If the man wanted to murder him, he could have already ambushed him at a stoplight or at some other time coming or going from his house or office.

Lieutenant Hara's jurisdiction ended several miles behind Gil's current position. If Gil confronted his tail in person and things got ugly, he wanted it to happen on Hara's turf.

Gil made a U-turn on the apron of a gas station and headed in the opposite direction. The man tailing him copied the move. When Gil passed back onto Lieutenant Hara's turf at the sign reading "City of Industry," he looked for some place to stop and meet this person.

By now, Gil's tail was following by little more than a car length and wore a grin that seemed painted on his face.

There were only two real choices: He could drive to the sheriff's station, in which case the man would drive away, or he could confront the man and try to learn what he was up to. The first choice might appear safer, but if the man had something to say—or do—to Gil, he would simply find another opportunity. The second choice carried the risk of immediate injury, but Gil was ready to take that risk. Better find out now than later.

Gil pulled into a mini mall with a convenience store, Chinese fast food restaurant, pizza parlor, real estate office, Chinese herb store, hair salon and dry cleaner. It seemed a public enough place to meet his tail and would have to do.

He deliberately chose a space with an empty slot alongside it. The person tailing him pulled up and stopped with enough of a skid to make the tires squeal. To Gil, that was the first sign of the man's intentions. Gil got out of his car and paused at his car's rear bumper. The other driver nearly leapt from his car, and walked briskly to within an arm's length from Gil, just within that invisible line that delineated Gil's space.

The man was about twenty-five years old. He wore a form-fitting tank top. His jeans were dressy and expensive, but his shoes were the cheap canvas slip-ons with white rubber soles often seen on older Asian immigrants. His muscles were highly defined, but appeared natural and enhanced by exercise rather than weights. His upper arms and what he could be seen of his chest and pectorals were tattooed with dragons and other Asian motifs, and some lettering that Gil recognized as Vietnamese even though he couldn't decipher it. His facial features were balanced and except for the deep red acne scars, he could have been described as handsome.

Clearly, he was a thug. Without question, he made his living by beating, extortion and intimidation and everything about him advertised his vocation. Gil had seen many such men in Saigon, but had only encountered them when they had approached him on the street with offers of drugs, contraband or a woman. In that setting, one simply ignored these men, who acted as pimps, drug, or currency dealers. This one, however, was not to be ignored. Gil couldn't just walk away from him, and certainly not after having initiated the confrontation himself.

"You Rodrigues?" The man had an accent. He pointed his index finger at Gil's chest. His tone was impudent.

"I am. And who might you be?" Gil's cheerfulness was fake and he advertised that fact with an obviously forced grin.

"I'm your worst nightmare." This time the man tapped Gil's

sternum. That physical contact released an initial drop of adrenaline into Gil's blood stream—that first drop that triggers a feeling of mild nausea. Then he felt his palms and the soles of his feet become damp, his heart rate and breathing increase.

Gil chuckled, but his tone became cold. "And from what film did you steal that line, Mr. Tank Top? Seems I've heard it before."

"I have a message for you. Stick to your business. Stay out of Chinese business and you will stay healthy."

"And who sent that message? Anyone I know?"

"Just stick to your business. That's all you need to know. I will help you remember." The man looked over both shoulders after he spoke. Gil anticipated a kick, but he was wrong.

What came at him was a straight jab that caught him above his left eye. He knew the punch had broken the skin over the eye and although the impact was sufficient to make him reel, Gil remained on his feet. He touched the wound reflexively, and saw blood on his hand. The pain and sight of his own blood only intensified Gil's anger.

Within seconds, Tank Top landed a roundhouse kick on Gil's right temple. A blow to the temple is capable of causing a knockout as the brain is shaken in its fluid cushion. Gil felt his knees buckle and felt a second wound open on the side of his head. Gil managed to stay conscious, but fell to his knees dazed.

Gil had his eyes on the man's midsection to gauge his next move, but Tank Top simply danced and shadowboxed while he taunted Gil. A grin remained on his face. That would be the man's mistake—not pressing his attack. Gil kept his eyes half-closed while he exaggerated a struggle to regain his footing.

Most people never forget how to ride a bike. The adrenaline that now dripped into Gil's blood stream called forth lethal skills buried deep in his motor cortex where they had lain unused for years. Gil had already found his legs, but swayed so as to appear in worse shape than he was. He tucked his chin to his chest. When he got to his feet, he continued reeling slightly and put his left arm out in a tentative, groping gesture, like a man feeling his way in a darkened room. The instant that Tank Top swatted it away, Gil put all his weight into a right cross that caught the man under his left eye. The power of the blow stunned the man severely and nearly knocked him unconscious. Tank Top had stepped back to shake off the blow, after which he stopped grinning and raised his own hands in front of him. "You won't do that again, Rodrigues," he said.

Maybe he miscalculated Gil's greater physical strength, height and weight. Maybe Gil's salt-and-pepper hair made the man overconfident. Maybe he would have been more cautious with a younger opponent. In any event, the man telegraphed his move by a half second—the half-second that can get you killed in a street fight or on a battlefield.

Gil was now fully alert and on his feet and he saw the barely perceptible little hop his assailant made on the ball of his right foot, before he thrust the edge of his left foot at Gil's head. Had the kick landed, Gil would have suffered severe facial and cranial damage, but Gil had seen it before; he knew it was coming. It was that little hop that tipped it off. It was the sucker punch of a chop suey street fighter who had trained in a gym, but never had to fight for his life.

Gil knew the defense. It was simple and effective. He made a half-turn to the right, leaned forward slightly and with his left forearm deflected the kick to the right away from his face and into the V formed by his right forearm and biceps. Instantly, he consolidated his hold by grabbing the man's pant leg with his left hand. Tank Top now had only his right leg for support, with Gil holding his left leg extended and trapped parallel to the ground.

The assailant's eyes were wide with shock; his face was seething with anger. "You got lucky, but you can't hold me all day, you old bastard! I'LL KILL YOU!"

The man tried to strike Gil's face and eyes, but the blows were easy to dodge because the man was so off-balance. He hopped slightly as if he were considering a drop kick with his right leg in an effort to free himself, but Gil's grip was solid and such a move would only land him on his back or his head.

Gil lowered the man's leg slightly allowing him to remain upright for reasons that would become painfully apparent to him in a moment.

"Temper, temper, my friend. Who sent you, grasshopper—or whatever your name is? Was it a man? A woman?"

The man screamed at Gil. "I DON'T KNOW WHAT YOU'RE TALKING ABOUT! I'M GONNA KILL YOU, BUT FIRST I'LL BREAK EVERY ONE OF YOUR RIBS AND FINGERS YOU OLD BASTARD!" The man's face had turned to crimson and his eyes were as wide as silver dollars.

"No, no, no, Grasshopper. You shouldn't call me 'old'. I'm very sensitive, you know, and you're hardly in a position to make threats."

With that, Gil delivered a brutal kick to the man's crotch, under the man's outstretched left leg, all the while preserving his hold on the leg. The kick missed the testicles, but struck the tailbone and root of his penis and sent a painful shock up the man's spine.

"Did they teach you this part at chop suey school, or whatever you idiots call it?" Gil delivered a second kick. This one was on target. The man screamed and turned pale. Few men reach adulthood without having been hit in the gonads either by accident or design, and they know that memorable feeling of seasickness and diarrhea combined. And some men don't know that sometimes the gonads swell from the trauma and have to be surgically removed.

"And one for good measure." Gil delivered a third kick. He then turned Tank Top's ankle inward so as to turn the man away from him and collapsed the man's supporting right leg from behind with a kick to the back of his knee. That move slammed Tank Top face-down into the asphalt. The man's impact with the ground drove the air from his lungs and he uttered a loud "uuaagh!"

By then Tank Top was losing consciousness. Gil dropped to his knees behind the now prostrate man to press the man's ankle into the base of his spine in a wrestling hold-down as old as the Bible. Gil then only had to wrap his left forearm around the man's forehead as he lay face down on the asphalt.

A small crowd had formed almost instantly from among the customers and storeowners. Someone ordered, "Dial 911!"

Gil could easily have held the man face down until the deputies had arrived, but his anger had turned to disgust and hatred. In all his life, he had never learned to laugh off physical threats. Rather than sustain his hold, he slid his left arm down over the man's throat. Then, with his right hand pressing on the back of the man's head, he formed a "sleeper" hold, one that blocked the blood flow through the carotid arteries to the brain, rendering the man unconscious for a few minutes. To be safe, however, Gil stood nearly on top of the man until the first of two patrol cars squealed into the mini-mall's parking lot, just feet from the two men.

Each car carried only one deputy. Both emerged with their hands on their guns, but did not draw them. Quickly they took in the scene. They looked at Gil, a white man in a blazer with blood on his face and clothes, but who otherwise appeared in charge, rational, and unarmed. Then they looked at the man lying face down with gang tattoos and the outline of something solid in his hip pocket. The one with corporal's stripes asked, "Is he dead or just out?"

"Just out." Gil pointed to the man's pocket. "That bulge in his hip pocket is a knife and most likely an illegal one, too."

"I'm way ahead of you," said the corporal as he removed a "butterfly" knife from the man's hip pocket.

One deputy moved swiftly to handcuff the man while the other felt his carotid artery for a pulse. “Yeah, he’s out all right. You look familiar,” he said, looking at Gil.

They patted the man down. His eyes, as he regained consciousness, widened in disbelief as he glared at Gil. They put him in the patrol car.

The corporal looked at Gil. “If looks could kill, eh? Do you have any weapons?”

“Don’t own any. Never did.” Gil held up his hands. “You’re welcome to pat me down, too. “

The corporal asked Gil to turn around and put his hands on the car roof after which he patted Gil down, but it was clear he was doing this for the record and didn’t really expect to find any weapons.

Gil felt his pulse and breathing return to normal as the adrenaline charge subsided. It was time to drop names. “You may have seen me with your Lieutenant Hara.” He pulled out his wallet and flashed his PI license at the corporal, who gave it only a cursory glance.

The corporal flicked the knife open and gingerly touched the blade. Even from several feet away, Gil could see it was razor sharp, its stiletto blade designed for slipping under a victim’s ribs to puncture the heart or aorta. “Bet this guy has a rap sheet a mile long. This blade alone is way over the legal size. We’ll need you to follow us to the station to make a report.”

At the sheriff’s station, Gil told the corporal about how the man was tailing him. No, he had never met the man in his life. No, he had no idea why he would tail him. Gil omitted the man’s warning to “stay out of Chinese business.”

“I’ve got to ask you,” the corporal said, “do you owe any money to sharks? Fooling around with other men’s wives? Why would this guy want to kick your ass?”

“No gambling debts, loan sharks, no wives of other men,” Gil said wearily, having no desire to get into his interest in David's murder. He told them about his work with insurance fraud instead.

"So you're saying it might be a revenge thing?" the corporal asked.

"Yeah, that's it. That's the ticket—a revenge thing." Gil would let it go at that. "Have to thank you guys for getting there so fast. Okay if I go now?"

Coming down off the adrenaline rush, Gil was beginning to feel sluggish. He had refused paramedic attention at the scene and had since rinsed off his wounds in the washroom. They might have needed stitches, but he didn't care at the moment.

The deputies released Gil with a warning that he would have to appear for the man's hearing on weapons and assault charges. The DA's office would handle that part.

"These guys with records almost always cop a plea, so I doubt if you'll ever have to testify at a trial," the corporal added.

As he walked to his car, Gil's anger was quiet, but intense. He now had two scores to settle: one for David, the other for himself.

CHAPTER TWENTY-THREE

The phone rang. It was Lieutenant Hara. "Where in hell did you learn that stuff? Or maybe I don't want to know."

"What stuff, Steve?"

"Sleeper holds and whatever else you did to that punk's testicles."

"Told you, Steve, I read a lot."

"I'm glad you never moved to the dark side, Gil. I never thought you were a pussy, but you never fail to surprise me. I've seen it take two and three men to subdue one of these guys on occasion. More if they're on PCP."

"I guess I should be flattered. Who is he?"

"He gave a common Vietnamese name, assuming it's real. He's most likely 'bui dui'."

"Boo who? Sounds Vietnamese, too."

"You guessed it, Gil. Southeast Asian gang member. I'm told it means 'dust in the wind'—some kind of poetic nonsense for the murder, mutilation, extortion and God knows what else these guys do. But that's what they call themselves."

"So it's their version of the 'Cosa Nostra'? Sounds like a bunch of poetic sadists. Has he given you any idea who hired him, Steve?"

"I couldn't pull that out of him with a rubber hose, even if it was legal. You can't imagine how tough these guys are. They won't even open up to their own lawyers when they do get prosecuted for something."

"Well, at least he's off the streets and I owe your guys a beer for the treatment they gave me."

"Gil, the other day you hinted at some sort of theory on your friend's murder. Got any more to tell me?"

"No. Still working on it."

Gil knew Lieutenant Hara was right about one thing: the sea would cover the Sahara before that thug told anyone who hired him. Those characters weren't freelancers; they needed the relative safety that went along with gang affiliation. Their bosses hired out guys like him on the expectation of absolute discretion and silence, and for him to talk would mark him for punishment by his own people.

After the fight with the thug, Gil had affected a stoical acceptance of all that transpired as he spoke with the deputies. Inside, however, he was enraged, and he knew that if he found the person who paid for this attack, he would do that person some serious injury. A smaller man or a man less competent in defending himself would now be in an intensive care ward and that thought simply fueled Gil's anger even more. He might have easily attributed the assault to someone out for revenge, arising out of one of his fraud investigations. The warning to "stay out of Chinese business," however, told him otherwise. It was time to move.

Gil had no desire to take a bullet in the base of his brain. He phoned Ming. "Meet me in the parking lot of the McDonald's on Gale Avenue on the side with the drive-up window. Be there at 5 P.M. Park front-end first and stand at the rear of your car facing the restaurant and the cars in the line for the drive-up."

Ming sounded unruffled. "This must be important."

"Oh, it is, Ming. Be there," Gil said and hung up.

McDonald's was a busy place at this time of day with a long line for the drive-up window. Two men talking in the well-lighted parking lot would be visible to a dozen persons at any one time.

Security cameras would pick up license plates. It wasn't a place to pull out a weapon and kill someone and Gil would feel relatively safe there.

Gil deliberately arrived five minutes late. There was Ming, as instructed. Ming offered his hand to Gil. Gil ignored it.

"I'm not here for games, Ming. I know you killed David. I know why and how. And by now you know I know."

Ming was at his urbane best. "Do I really, Mr. Rodrigues? And you took all these precautions because you thought I would kill you? Really now."

"I'm certain the gun used to kill David will never be found, but a second one is easy enough to come by."

Ming affected a disappointed look. "I believe you and I have what people in your culture call a 'personality clash'. I know you don't like me, but that doesn't make me a murderer."

"Your personality clash with David—not with me—started it all. David was honest, moralistic—even prudish. Theft and corruption went against his ethics. In character, he was your opposite in every way imaginable."

Ming's tone was conciliatory. "I agree, David was certainly strait-laced and steeped in those silly doctrines of that obese and ancient sage, but … "

Gil interrupted. "You didn't like him, and I'm sure he didn't like you either. It annoyed you that one of your bosses in China made you hire David because of his *guanxi*. You hoped he would quit if you made his life miserable enough with demeaning errands and busy work. Then you flaunted your theft by making him pay those invoices to your phony companies."

"Theft? Taken something that's not mine, you say?"

Gil's voice took on a hard edge. "I know about all your fictitious business names and you now know I've seen the books of DaleeAhn—the books that document your embezzlement. And that's why you killed David."

Ming's facial expression changed to one of alarm. His pupils widened. His Adam's apple bobbed as he swallowed. His voice, however, remained calm. "You're making this up."

"Am I? David had not one, but two sets of the company records at his house. The set you took from him on the night you killed him was a duplicate. You were taking a chance no one would look at his hard drive at his home after he died. David was a good accountant. Good for me, but bad for you was the fact that he was also a computer geek. He backed up everything."

Ming's arrogance began to return just when Gil thought it might begin to crumble. "Let's assume he has copies of our books. You still haven't—what's the expression?—'made the case' against me for murder."

"Yes, our courts do have a higher standard of proof than in your country. Most of the time we don't extract confessions from innocent people. But it gets better."

"'Better', you say?" Ming's voice was controlled, but Gil could see he was taking breaths just ever so much faster.

"And, I know about the work you do for your CIA—or your MSS—or whatever it's called in China. Our Customs people will be interested in that operation with illegal exports like machine tools and patented medical products. I'm guessing that was your main mission, but you found a great opportunity to line your pockets with the People's money."

"My, Mr. Rodrigues, you have done your homework."

"And David either didn't understand or didn't care about your purchases of restricted export items. He just wanted to be accorded some respect and a better paycheck."

"You did know David longer than I did," Ming said.

"I know other things, too. Our FBI will be interested in your attempts to recruit people like Sabrina who work in defense projects."

"You do know things, it now appears, but you still haven't told me why or how I'd commit murder."

"David could be naïve. He would know you and Quon at the consulate were buddies. Maybe he even knew that you were classmates at that college in Beijing where they train diplomats and sadists. What he didn't know is just how close you two were."

"And just how close is that, Mr. Rodrigues?"

"I said I know other things. I know that your father and his both took a bullet in the neck for stealing the Chinese people's money. That means you, Liao and he all knew the risks you were taking—you by stealing, they by sharing the take with you. Whatever success you had stealing technology wouldn't save your skins if you got caught."

"No, David wouldn't know that."

Gil pressed on. "David was impressed with Quon's polished exterior. He thought Quon had some kind of oversight or influence with you, so that he simply had to have a heart-to-heart chat with Quon and show him the evidence of your theft and Quon would make things right. Finally, Quon agreed to meet David at the temple, but then he called you instead and told you that you had a problem that needed fixing."

"And I just went and killed him?"

"Yes, but not in the parking lot. Too messy. Too many possible witnesses. Frankly, I don't think Quon thought you'd kill David. He thought you'd just appease him in some way to keep him quiet—throw him a bone in the form of a raise or cut him in on the action. But you had had your fill of this quiet little man you hated because he was just about everything you weren't. And you had been used to putting guys like David in their place back in China with your electric truncheons and God knows what. So you had Liao, your stooge and partner, drive you to the temple parking lot, where you met David who never imagined you were there to kill him."

"That's all speculation on your part, Mr. Rodrigues."

"Is it? You got hold of a .22 handgun. That's easy enough for someone with your background. If you couldn't buy one that couldn't be traced to you, you could have a gun shipped in a diplomatic pouch to Quon. That too, would be easy for an MSS man to arrange. You told David you and he needed privacy. You had him drive you a couple of blocks away and park under the shadow of that big eucalyptus while Liao followed."

"You will need witnesses."

"Oh, I have witnesses. You knew David was carrying company records in his briefcase because he thought he would be meeting your friend Quon."

"This is speculation, Mr. Rodrigues."

"Is it? You're left-handed, aren't you Ming?"

Ming's eyes widened again. He didn't answer, but he glanced at his left hand as if Gil had revealed some great secret about it.

"That means that it wasn't all that awkward for you to press the muzzle of your weapon to the base of David's brain from your place on the passenger seat. And your masters taught you well. You knew David's flesh would act as a silencer when you pulled the trigger."

"And you think I'd confess to anything like this to your Lieutenant Hara?"

"Frankly, no, at least not in this country and under our system."

"So we're both patriots of sorts, aren't we, Mr. Rodrigues? We're both products of our political systems." Ming's tone was factual and not ironic.

"I have to confess, Ming, there is one thing I haven't figured out yet and it makes my blood boil."

Now Ming's tone was sarcastic. "That's suddenly modest of you. I can't imagine anything you haven't figured out."

"That Vietnamese hoodlum. Who sent him after me?"

Ming looked down and shook his head. His face showed genuine disgust. "I'm ashamed to say our colleague Mr. Liao boasted to me about arranging that without my knowledge or permission. He was so proud of himself, but it was stupid because it further focused your attention on us. I was furious and made him return to China. That's not my—style? Is that the word? I believe that's how you say it."

"But how could he know I was digging around, or that I suspected you two?"

"He didn't. Liao jumped to a conclusion—a conclusion that turned out to be correct."

"I'm afraid I still don't follow you."

"The day you visited our offices. Liao noticed the key to the rear door was missing from the rack near the lavatory. He knew you had to pass the key rack to use the lavatory, but wasn't sure if you had taken the key or he had merely mislaid it about the office somewhere."

Gil finished for Ming. "And when he found the key back on the rack the next morning, he knew I must have snooped around your offices and warehouse the night before."

"Yes. And then when I told him you refused to work for us, he panicked and that's when I suggested he go back to China. He said we needed to teach you a lesson. I thought he had more sense, but like a fool, and without telling me, he paid that young man to scare you off. It was a stupid and desperate thing to do. You and I are professionals and for what it may be worth, I'm embarrassed by such impulsive clumsiness."

"You know, I believe you on that item. But beneath your mask of refinement is a man capable of murder—and worse. I like to remind myself that the man in charge of torture in Cambodia was a Ph.D. And what's really rich is that the evidence needed to convict you of murder isn't strong enough—not here anyway—even though you and I know you did it—how and why. I've no positive ID."

"Are you telling me you don't plan to seek retribution for what I ... " Ming caught himself. "For this murder you say I committed?"

"I never said that. But you can be convicted of other things—federal raps like attempted espionage and exporting restricted items," Gil said.

"And you've spoken to your federal people?"

"No, I haven't talked to Customs or the FBI yet, so maybe you ought to think about heading back to China before I tell those folks what I know. To keep my license—and maybe even avoid prosecution for concealing evidence—I'll have to tell them, but it doesn't have to be today—or even before you leave."

"Again, and for what it may be worth, Mr. Rodrigues, I underestimated you, if only for a short while, yet I cannot believe a man like you would not seek revenge."

"You have a chance to run. Better use it while you can," Gil said matter-of-factly.

Ming said nothing, but stared directly into Gil's eyes for some hint of deception. "Why do I not trust you?"

Gil changed the subject. "Ming, you and I have at least three things in common. We value personal loyalty, we've both been small fry in the secret world, and we're both capable of violence. We've seen the betrayal and cruelty that's so much a part of our world in this century. And, on a personal note, I think we're both old enough to know who we are. The difference is that I changed that person when I discovered him and didn't like what I saw. You didn't."

"Don't tell me you didn't enjoy being part of an elite?"

"When I was young and dumb, yes, but at this point in life I couldn't care less about cloak and dagger nonsense. The prime difference between you and me is that you make no distinction between those who deserve killing and those who don't. Men like you do it for the fun—for the power."

"Saying all this makes you feel morally superior, doesn't it, Mr. Rodrigues?"

"No doubt, yes. I wouldn't say it otherwise. But some of us did draw the line and paid a price for it when we did."

"But someone has to do the killing." Ming stated it as a fact. "Where I come from we have to maintain order and provide food for well over a billion people. That requires order. Most people are sheep, so food comes first in my part of the world. We let others worry about their souls and spiritual life—whatever that is. It's no accident that your notions of freedom and civil liberties came out of the west, not from the east."

"We agree there, Ming. I live in the real world—or try to. It's just that some of you become monsters with your power over life and death. You love it and you showed how much you love it in your own country. My sources have confirmed that much for me."

"I did my job in keeping order among 1.2 billion people."

"And men like you are always just doing your job. The guy who dropped the blade on the guillotine was just doing his job. Men like you will buy into any ideology, no matter how repulsive, if it means holding on to that job with the power and freedom to commit the unspeakable acts that go with it."

"Oh come now, Mr. Rodrigues, I thought we agreed that someone has to do the world's dirty work?"

"There are limits even to the dirty work, but I guess if it's not you doing it, it's someone else. I just happened to stumble on to your game. But you burned my friend David—as much out of irrational personal hatred as anything else—and that I won't forgive."

"I plan to return to China within days. I have an open ticket."

"So I understand. I won't try to stop you." Gil looked at Ming, touched his index finger to his forehead and walked to his car.

He drove to his office. There he had everything he needed to settle the score for David.

CHAPTER TWENTY-FOUR

Ming hired a temp to answer the phone at DaleeAhn and to serve as a live presence until someone else took over or the business was shut down. The temp's duties were trivial at this point. She spoke English with a heavy accent. She was also wary. She gave Gil Ming's flight information only after he told her that he was Ming's immigration attorney and he had to see him before his departure, that it was urgent. Ming had forgotten a vital travel document and if he didn't get it before boarding his plane, he might be prevented from re-entering China. She bought the story. Gil called the airline to confirm the scheduled departure. He didn't want to arrive early.

Gil found Ming at the small bar lounge at the Tom Bradley International Terminal at LAX. He was sitting on a barstool at one of the fixed pedestal tables that stand at bar height.

"Ah, Mr. Rodrigues, I'm shocked to see you here." He scanned the crowd anxiously. "I judged you to be a man of your word. So you went to the authorities with your theory, after all."

"I *am* a man of my word. There's no one here with a warrant for your arrest. I'll talk to Hara and the feds after you're back in China."

"Then why did you take the trouble?"

"I expect this'll be the last time I see you."

"You predict such things, do you?"

"I know a good bet when I see one."

"I'll be boarding shortly. These international flights involve so much dead time, but perhaps you'll let me buy you a drink." He signaled the cocktail waitress. "A martini as I recall, Mr. Rodrigues?"

Gil nodded to the waitress.

"I bear you no malice," Ming said, "but to be frank I have sensed an animosity in you towards me from the beginning."

"That's an understatement if there ever was one. I know that you killed David. I've already told you why and how. I'm not here to cover that again."

The waitress set Gil's drink down with the tab. Ming snatched it up, looked at the amount and covered it with a twenty-dollar bill.

Gil raised his glass in a toast. Ming raised his, but looked puzzled. "Just what are we toasting?"

"Do we need an excuse to drink?" Gil asked. He glanced upward as if in thought. "You mentioned the dead time on international flights. Let's toast the dead time."

As Gil had seen so many times with Asians, Ming touched Gil's glass to make a clinking sound and smiled weakly. "To the dead time."

"To the dead time." Gil swallowed half of his drink.

"That's the boarding call for my flight. I must go now."

Gil held out a sealed manila envelope and made a conciliatory smile. "I brought you some reading material for the flight. It is a nonstop, is it not?" Gil offered the envelope.

Ming took it from Gil. He looked puzzled as he hefted it and felt its contents through the buff paper. Then he dropped it into his briefcase without thanking Gil. "We don't stop before China -- we fly straight to Shanghai, then to Beijing. Why would you ask?"

"Just checking."

"Goodbye, Mr. Rodrigues. I believe it is passengers only in the international boarding area here in Los Angeles. Perhaps we'll meet again."

"I'll see you in hell." Gil's tone was flat. It communicated no anger and no irony. It was just a statement.

Ming said nothing, but Gil detected a flash of suspicion in his eyes and Gil had to hope he hadn't given his play away by appearing smug or triumphant. Gil stood and watched Ming's back as he rode the escalator to the departure gates. At the top of the escalator, Ming looked over his shoulder without breaking his stride.

He and Gil made eye contact. Gil gave Ming a curt smile and touched his forehead with his forefinger. Gil ordered a second martini and sat facing the escalators to the departure area. Then he watched the display board until he was sure Ming's plane was airborne.

Ming's flight was at cruising altitude. The first of two in-flight movies had been shown and the attendants were serving a second round of drinks and refreshments. Ming had fallen asleep from the combination of fatigue, boredom and alcohol. He awoke suddenly and explosively as one does from a nightmare. He made a loud "ah!" sound, startling the man next to him as he did so. He composed himself and apologized in both Mandarin and English to the passenger, an elderly man with silver hair. "I must have been dreaming. I'm sorry."

If he could have seen his own face, he would have seen it was ashen and he would have seen small beads of sweat on his forehead. He blotted the sweat with the cocktail napkin.

He nearly lunged for his briefcase under the seat, once more startling the old man next to him. He smiled weakly at the man and, through an act of will, slowed his movements as he put the briefcase on his lap and opened it. He stopped a flight attendant and asked for their estimated arrival time. "About eight hours more," she said.

Hurriedly, Ming removed Gil's envelope from his briefcase. It contained nearly an inch of paper with a cover letter. He fanned the stack with his thumb and index finger and then closed his eyes in disbelief for a full half-minute after which he took a long, deep breath and began reading the cover letter. He stopped about midway in the letter and glanced nervously at the old man beside him to see if he might be looking over his shoulder. He again flipped through the enclosures looking at sections randomly.

They were copies of the DaleeAhn books and the fictitious business registrations in Ming's name. Ming laid his two hands flat on the bundle as if not being able to see it would make it disappear. He returned to the cover letter because it was this, as much as the enclosures, that caused his heart rate and breathing to speed up and beads of sweat to appear on his forehead.

The letter was on Gil's professional letterhead. The copies smelled of toner and were on common copy paper with the images reduced to fit 8 1/2 x 11 sheets. The letter's indicia made it clear that Gil had shipped this package to China by international air carrier twenty-four hours prior. Ming's flight would take at least seventeen hours, so the package would be in Beijing when he arrived there, but it wouldn't make any difference if it arrived earlier or later. It would arrive. Ming reread the letter, this time more slowly.

Gentlemen:

In the United States, the fraudulent diversion of company funds for personal use is a form of embezzlement and a crime. Such a crime is punishable by fines or imprisonment or both. I am certain it is also a crime in your country, punishable by imprisonment at best or by death at worst.

The documentary evidence enclosed represents a significant portion of the accounting records of the DaleeAhn Corporation and the personal bank and credit card account statements of Zhiyuan (Jeff) Ming. These records show that he, Mr. Ming, the CEO of DaleeAhn Corporation, a subsidiary of The COI Corporation in China, has misappropriated company funds, converted company property, falsified expense reports and generally diverted company monies to his personal bank accounts. These documents show that he accomplished this largely through the use of fictitious business entities that exist only on paper and only to open the bank accounts through which he filtered his stolen funds.

I anticipate that, in his defense, Mr. Ming will declare these documents to be forgeries. For that reason, and in the interest of justice, I expect that you will verify the validity of my charges and the authenticity of these documents. You can do this in one or both of two ways: First, you can send your own forensic accountant or corporate auditor to the U.S. to audit the company financial records. Secondly, you can hire an American accounting firm to perform an independent, forensic audit. My own estimate is that Mr. Ming has stolen at least US$900,000 of the money funded by the People's Republic of China through the Bank of China and COI, DaleeAhn's parent corporation. No other conclusion can be drawn from an independent audit of these records. I will, of course, turn this documentary evidence over to American law enforcement authorities.

I should add that I am also aware of violations of U.S. export laws in the illegal export of restricted export products. I will also bring those activities to the attention of our Customs and FBI officials.

Dewei Liao, Mr. Ming's colleague, was clearly complicit in these acts of embezzlement, but I have no concern for his involvement or fate for reasons you will infer. I believe he has already returned to China.

You are, of course, entitled to know how I came into possession of these records and my motive in bringing them to your attention.

First, regarding how I came to possess these records: Until his murder, David Chang was the accounting manager of DaleeAhn Corporation, as your own records will show. Mr. Chang and his family were neighbors and close friends of mine. He and his wife became American citizens after having emigrated from China nearly two decades ago.

After David's murder, his daughter asked me to do what I could as a private investigator to find the person or persons who murdered her father. Our local law enforcement authorities are generally competent, but have not found sufficient evidence for a successful prosecution under our criminal justice system in which the burden of proof lies with the state. In my efforts to identify David's murderer, his widow and daughter gave me free access to David's home office, his computer, and his files.

Moreover, I have identified the fictitious business names that appear in accounts payable documents. That those company names were created and are owned solely by Mr. Ming is a matter of public record open to anyone at the Los Angeles County Recorder's Office in Norwalk, CA.

I am not an accountant, but it became immediately obvious that David Chang had been keeping an extra set of DaleeAhn accounting records in his home office.

These documents show how Mr. Ming stole company funds. Kept secretly by Mr. Chang, they reveal how the company funds were actually spent and will make it clear to any objective examiner that the officers of DaleeAhn have committed a form of larceny under any system of laws.

Secondly, regarding my motives in bringing this matter to your attention: I assume you have been informed of David Chang's murder even though Mr. Chang was an American citizen. He was, after all, the accounting manager of

DaleeAhn. I am now certain that Jeff Ming murdered David Chang, but I do not have the kind of evidence that would support a conviction of murder in an American court of law. Mr. Ming is so confident of that fact that he impliedly confessed the crime to me in private, and in the absence of witnesses or recording device. Either he did not know that that David kept a duplicate set of corporate financial records in his home or, if he did know, he hoped that they would not come to light after his death. It is these records that will support my charges of embezzlement. I am also certain that Mr. Ming stole copies of these records from David on the night he murdered David. David's survivors and I found these duplicates on David's computer and in his home office files.

Of course, David's family and I would like to see Mr. Ming punished for the murder of David. Failing that, however, if I can cause Jeff Ming to be punished for embezzlement and related crimes in his homeland, then perhaps David Chang and his survivors will have been served an equitable measure of justice.

I will have given a sealed envelope containing copies of this letter and its enclosures to Mr. Ming before he boards his flight to China. In doing so, I am taking the risk of his reading them before boarding and possibly aborting his return. I am gambling, however, that the combination of his arrogance and the bustle and haste of boarding will cause him to read these documents only after it is too late for him to avoid justice in China. Of course, I need not give him copies, but the thought of him reading and effectively delivering them on his nonstop flight gives me great satisfaction. Moreover, and until his end, I want him to know that it was I, with the help of David Chang and his survivors, who brought him to justice.

Should it come to it, I will be pleased to discuss this matter with your representative(s) here in the U.S., but only in the presence of member(s) of our law enforcement agencies.

Yours truly,

Gilberto J. Rodrigues

The cover letter revealed that Gil had addressed and shipped a copy of the package separately to each of three persons: the director of the Bank of China, the Minister of State Security, and the CEO of China Overseas Investments Corporation, DaleeAhn's nominal parent company. Ming knew that none of the three men could refuse to act on the letter and its contents without putting himself at risk of being charged with nonfeasance or even collusion.

The three would be compelled to act if only for their own safety, and Ming knew that meant only one thing: He was reading his own death warrant six miles over the Pacific Ocean. Barely keeping his panic under control, Ming began reading the letter from the beginning again in the vague hope of finding something on which to hang a challenge and defense.

Ming's mind raced. Damn! If he had only opened the envelope before boarding the aircraft. He considered faking a medical emergency in the hope of forcing a return to Los Angeles, but the probability of a physician being on board a full flight was very high and he would spot the deception. Furthermore, the flight was past the midpoint.

Ming knew that meant he literally, and now symbolically, had passed the point of no return. He had to think, because it was possible that they would arrest him and take his luggage and briefcase when he deplaned in China. But then Ming realized it would make little difference whether he was arrested that night, the following night, next week or next month. He would be arrested and in China, no attorney would be present at such an interrogation.

Yes, Ming would swear that the documents had to be forgeries, but his interrogators would know differently. He hadn't just padded his expense account; he had stolen large sums of the People's money, and whatever status and privilege he might have enjoyed as an MSS agent before his mission to the U.S. wouldn't protect him from prosecution. The director of the Bank of China would know, the boss of his parent company would know, and the head of MSS would know, too. A package that was sent by international air courier with a private investigator's name listed as sender on the air bill was not something that the offices of the three men could ignore.

Ming, of all people, would know how confessions were obtained in China. He would hope for a prison sentence, but he knew the likely penalty, and he knew of the Chinese custom of parading the condemned, their arms bound and in open trucks, to the killing ground. He knew also that because of his relative youth, his heart, skin, liver, kidneys and corneas would be "harvested" minutes after his execution for transplant into the living. What was left of his body would be wrapped in gauze, mummy-like, before his executioners disposed of it.

Hours before Ming read Gil's letter in flight, Gil drove home over the Santa Monica and Pomona freeways. He punched his car radio to an "oldies" station and drummed on his steering wheel to the beat of rock 'n' roll from the fifties and sixties. At times he sang along with such gusto that he drew looks from other drivers.

What Ming didn't know—nor would he care if he did know—was that Gil had arranged for a messenger service to drop off a copy of the poison pen letter and package at Lieutenant Hara's office the following day.

Gil would sleep well that night, even knowing that in the next day or two, he would have to recap everything for Hara and the feds. He dreaded the thought. He was sick of it all, but he wanted to get it over with so he could get back to a routine of sorts. He decided on the spot to invite Diana to Las Vegas for a couple of days. "Yes, that'll be fun," he thought, "she's a knockout in a cocktail dress." He would call her when he finished with Hara and the feds.

CHAPTER TWENTY-FIVE

Whatever gratification Gil felt in solving David's murder and trumping Hara had already faded by the next day. Gil had no desire to gloat or rub it in. Sabrina, after all, tipped him off in the beginning. Her instincts turned out to be sound. He felt confident that he and Hara would remain friends for a long time.

Hara waited hours after he read the letter before calling Gil. Gil credited the delay to Hara's need to digest it all and to come up with his own report that would leave the case as officially unsolved, but with the new prime suspect as beyond extradition.

The package wasn't even in sight when Gil stopped by Hara's office. Gil's game plan was to be gracious in victory because he expected Hara to be defensive—and defensive he was.

"I never did get to talk with Quon at the consulate," Hara said. "They stalled me for days and finally told me he's back in China, too. And if the Johnson kid could have made a positive ID, I'd have busted Ming right away."

"Yes, you would have had the same track to run on as did I." Gil didn't want to patronize, but Hara seemed to be getting more comfortable.

"Of course," Hara said. "They'll just assume Quon was sharing in the take."

Gil told Hara everything—or nearly everything—and continued to put it all in a context of dumb luck. He lied about nothing, except his having let himself into the warehouse after stealing the key. He said that he had examined David's books, visited Quon, the library, and the murder site all on casual hunches or suggestions from Sabrina.

"And that's it, Steve. I'm tired of thinking and talking about it. I don't have your expertise in homicide. I just got lucky." Hara suppressed a smile, but Gil spotted it and maintained a disarming manner. "If you don't mind, Steve, I sure as hell don't feel like talking to the feds today, so give it a rest for a day or so. Besides, Ming and his flunky aren't here anyway."

"That shouldn't be a problem," Hara said.

"Customs will nail the freight forwarders and seize those goods still on the dock," Gil said. "We can be sure these shippers are working with others who are also exporting restricted items."

"But our murderer got away from us," Hara said.

"From us, Steve, but only from us." The two men grinned at each other.

The lieutenant arranged for Customs and FBI agents to meet Gil in Hara's office at the sheriff's station. Although the feds talked down to Gil, he was relieved that it didn't turn out to be an ordeal. It was plain they regarded private investigators as a form of life low in the food chain and not very bright, to boot. That was all right with Gil. They could regard him as a half-wit for all he cared at that point.

Gil stayed with his story of having spotted some items in the DaleeAhn warehouse strictly by accident, and his consequent suspicions of Ming and his subsequent investigative actions. After interviewing Gil, the federal agents implied that they had bigger fish to fry, and with Ming back in China, his U.S. operation had been effectively shut down anyway. Gil thought it unlikely he would hear from the feds again.

***

Ten weeks had passed since David's murder. Lieutenant Hara saw it first in the *Los Angeles Times* and called Gil at his office. His voice conveyed utter astonishment.

"Jeez! Have you seen today's *Times* yet?"

"No, Steve, not yet. What's up—Japan apologized for Pearl Harbor?"

"Wise ass. But it may be even better than that. I don't ever want to make an enemy of you, guy."

"Hell, Steve, what'd I do?"

"Looks like Ming bought the farm—Chinese style. It's in the international news section."

Gil found the paper with Rose in the reception area of his office building. He stood while he opened it to the right page.

"China Executes Corrupt Officials," read the headline of a wire service story labeled as "Special To The Times." But it was the photo and caption that riveted Gil's attention. The picture had been taken in a Chinese courtroom and credited to Reuters. There stood Jeff Ming, without a tie, and wearing a worsted blazer and a shirt with a standing collar that gave him a clerical look. He could have been taken for a Protestant minister. His face was impassive, displaying neither fear nor shock. Standing on each side of him, at attention, were uniformed policemen wearing officers' shoulder pips. The caption said that Ming was executed for corruption hours after the photo was taken.

The background text related how an ongoing, massive anti-corruption campaign in China had resulted in hundreds of executions in the prior year alone. The Chinese government, according to the story, faced a dilemma: Its ranks were rife with corruption, but it could not purge that corruption too ruthlessly because it had to rely on those very officials to maintain its rule. So, the story pointed out, the regime would selectively shoot people as a warning to others—"killing a chicken to scare the monkeys," as a Chinese saying put it.

Two sentences in particular caught Gil's attention: "Dewei Liao and Shilin Quon, convicted as Ming's co-conspirators, are to be sentenced in a separate hearing." The second said, "Ming and

Liao operated a business in Southern California prior to their recent return to China."

Gil sat on the couch in the reception area. He wasn't looking at the photo any more, but was just sitting quietly.

Gil recalled a line he heard in some TV drama: "Revenge is a dish best served cold. "

Gil's exultation, though, was tempered by a sense of letdown, too. He had unmasked David's killer and contrived a punishment that fit the crime—a bullet in the base of the brain. At the same time, however, he had no real feeling of finality and certainly none of closure. He had learned that word was empty psychobabble with little connection with human emotion.

Back in his office, Gil phoned Sabrina. "He's dead."

"I'm sorry, Uncle Gil—who's dead?" Gil kept quiet. Sabrina paused and then gasped audibly. "You mean that creep who killed my dad?"

"Yes, honey. Ming. They shot him for stealing the People's money. And I wouldn't bet on a comfortable old age for Quon and Liao, either."

"Ming was shot for stealing money—not for killing my dad?" Her voice rose. "For stealing money?"

"Yes, for stealing money, but he's just as dead. You do remember that none of us get out of this world alive? We live once, we die once."

"I wish he could have been tried here. Happening over there, it's almost like he got away with it."

"In a perfect world, honey, we'd have perfect justice, but we don't live in a perfect world. That means we have to settle for imperfect justice sometimes and sometimes no justice at all." Gil felt the disparity in their ages acutely at that moment. "I did the best I could," he added.

There was another pause before Sabrina spoke again. "I can't say I'm sorry in the least—he deserved it for what he did. I'm glad he's dead, but I wish none of this ever had to happen."

"But we can't undo what's done, even though neither he nor your dad had to die this way," Gil said.

"Mom, Aunt Diana and I will all feel better now that Ming's been punished, but I don't think Dad ever wanted to hurt him," Sabrina said.

"Nor do I, honey. But Ming treated your dad like dirt. David only wanted to be treated the way he treated others—with some dignity. Out of resentment, your dad decided to blow the whistle on him, but he had no idea of Ming's background, ruthlessness, or capacity for violence."

"Yes, Dad could be naïve in a lot of ways," Sabrina said.

"And I don't know if your dad knew or understood the spy part of Ming's operation. I think it was the theft and embezzlement that appalled him. After all, how many people would understand something like restricted export items? I know I didn't."

"Yes, that would all be beyond my dad's experience."

"Your dad's naïve belief that Quon would make things right cost him his life."

"But you know, Unc, the more I think of my dad, the more I think … " She paused.

Gil finished for her. "That he would have forgiven his killer?"

"Yes," she said, "I like to think he would."

"He would have, honey, but I wouldn't have, and neither would you."

EPILOGUE

When Gil's kids called, they dropped hints that significant others had come into their lives and asked Gil to keep his fingers crossed. He told them that the news made him happy, and they knew it did.

Diana, however, was a concern. Gil hadn't heard from her in over two weeks. When she failed to return his calls to her home, he became alarmed and called the hospital twice. Both times they said she was in the O.R. and took a message, but she never called him back. Gil knew what that meant. He would call her no more. He would wait for her call—a call he knew would come.

It was late in the afternoon when she phoned Gil at his office. Would it be okay if she stopped by? Gil agreed, knowing it would be futile to ask her to meet him for drinks. Gil met her under the breezeway at the side entrance of his office building. He didn't want her in his drab monk's cell.

"Gil, this is the hardest thing I've ever had to say."

"Women usually say that just before they dump a guy."

"I'll cry if you use that word. It's so cruel. Let's just say I—we—it's time we moved on."

"Moved on or dumped on—the result is the same. But you do what you have to do. We'll have a lot to remember."

"Gil—I'm not going away mad. You do know that, don't you? You'll always occupy a special place with me."

"I could have had more faith."

"Faith?" Diana looked puzzled.

"I should have shown more faith in you when Hara said you—and I—were under suspicion. I have to confess Steve nearly persuaded me that you might have had the motive and means to have your brother murdered. It goes with the job, I guess. I'm truly sorry."

She pressed against him and held his face in her hands. Her eyes were moist. "Please, please—you have nothing to be sorry for. Don't blame yourself. I could never have put myself back together without you."

"And you did the same for me." He kissed her forehead. "Let's not forget it was David who brought us together."

"It was. He knew it would work." She flashed a thin smile. "Until the wounds healed, anyway."

Gil forced a smile, too. "It's been nice." He paused. "It brought us back among the living. Now it's part of whoever we are."

"I like that—a passage affair." She chuckled. "Makes it sound—like a film title."

Gil looked into her eyes. "Do you have plans? I'm no expert, but I'd guess you're young enough to go forth and multiply."

"I think I am, but if I can't pop one on my own, I'll adopt."

Gil winked at her. "Babies are good. There were moments when I wished you were fifteen years older—or, better yet—I was fifteen years younger." He grinned. "I might have been inclined if I hadn't been fixed."

"And you would have gotten away with it, too. But then you would have had to marry me." She laughed, looked skyward, and put her hand over her heart. "To save my honor, good sir."

Gil feigned indignation. "*Your* honor? What about mine—or what's left of it? Speaking of which, good lady, why do I think there's another man offstage?"

She looked down and stepped away from him. "There's a doctor at the hospital. He's a vascular surgeon. I work with him a lot in the O.R. That type of work can draw people together."

"A new romance?" Gil raised his eyebrows.

"Let's say he's showing strong interest. Doctors don't have the time for elaborate courtship games. They get right down to business. I guess men feel their own biological clocks, too."

"Who's the lucky guy?"

"He's American-born, but his parents came from Taiwan."

"That's good, too. You deserve a younger man—younger and successful—to take care of you while the babies are young."

She wrapped her arms around Gil's chest and pressed her ear against his shoulder. "You know I'd never hurt you."

"When Helen's condition went south, I knew I'd lose her sooner rather than later. I just didn't know when sooner would come. But I was ready by then. And I knew that you, too, would go away in time."

"You knew?" Diana seemed surprised.

"The sweet part ends in time. It always does. If you keep that in mind, it doesn't hurt so much." There was no anger, no self-pity, and no lament in Gil's voice.

"And I've no regrets," she said.

"What's to regret, pretty lady?"

There was a moment of silence. Diana spoke first. Her eyes were wide. Her voice conveyed an earnestness and her words came fast.

"When she's old enough—I want a girl first—I'll tell her about us." Her smile said she was pleased with her promise.

Gil winked at her. "Don't forget now, these stories need to grow in the telling. All families need their folklore, so be sure to embroider it." He paused. "Make it Bogey and Bergman and The Long Goodbye."

"I'll make it a Harlequin Romance. Will that do?"

"Cast me in the Bogey version if you don't mind."

"I always knew you were a romantic. They grow up fast, you know—especially the girls." She gave him a coquettish grin. "She'll have to fill in some details."

"She'll be a beauty. They're nice when they're small. I can't wait to push her on a swing. I'll spoil her rotten."

"I hope that's a promise—*Uncle* Gil." Diana presented her cheek for Gil to kiss. Then she turned and, without a word or backward glance, was gone. He watched her walk to her car and drive off in the warm California sun. They made eye contact as she left the lot, but neither waved.

By then it was nearly five and Gil decided that it was late enough in the day for a martini. He drove to the Sunset Room, the feel of Diana's skin still on his lips. He knew he would never see her again, despite her promise. Women don't introduce former lovers to their husbands unless they chance upon them in public. When that does happen, they try to pass them off as acquaintances, but the husbands know otherwise. The eyes give it away.

"But maybe it's better that way," he thought. "Yes, it is. It's better to never see them again. It's better to remember them as they were then, in the sweet time, when it was new and when time let you play."

To Gil's mind, two things were now right in the world: Ming had paid the price for David's murder and Diana found the urge to brood. Gil took credit for the former. After some thought, he took credit for the latter, too. Now if his own kids added members to society that would be nice, too. But he wouldn't take credit for that.

Jesse the bartender was in the last hour of his shift and was clearly fretting about something. He had the races on all three TVs and was chewing on a pencil because he wasn't allowed to smoke behind the bar. The condition of the pencil told Gil that he had put a bundle on a race, but his horse hadn't finished in the money.

Jesse took the pencil from his mouth. "You're a little early today, Gil. The usual?"

"The usual, Jesse—no, make it a margarita."

"Celebrating?"

"Sort of."

Jesse placed the drink in front of Gil and again took the pencil from his mouth. "So, how's life been treating you?"

Gil looked past Jesse and into space without saying a word for so long that he made the man uneasy. He took a long sip of his drink. After that and a long smile, Gil Rodrigues spoke. "Pretty good, Jesse. Pretty damn good."

THE END